TRIDEVI TRIDENT

(INSPIRED BY TRUE INCIDENTS)

ABOUT THE AUTHOR

Ahmed Sayeed is a simple man, retired from the office of the Accountant General Hyderabad, He completed his Ph.D. and LL.B after retirement at the age of 70. He does not believe Creation was caused by any God or super Spirit since no animal including human being have a spirit called "Soul" It is the activity of our brain that every animal including humans possess. That is the thing that make Humans a "Social Animal" or "Intelligent Animal."

He believes the theory of Evolution of Natural selection which was first propounded by Charles Darwin in his Book "On the Origin of Species" in 1859, and is the process by which organs change overtime and as a result of change inheritable.

He also believes that there is no necessity of any God to take up creation and thereby expect man or woman to prostrate before him for life time. If any man has a desire to submit and give Credit to him it is nothing other than human emotion. It is not a God but human itself. And this connotes that the Religion and God are the creations of human for tackling his fear and ambition.

TRIDEVI TRIDENT

(INSPIRED BY TRUE INCIDENTS)

Dr. AHMED SAYEED

ZORBA BOOKS

2018

Published in India by Zorba Books, 2018

Website: www.zorbabooks.com
Email: info@zorbabooks.com

Print Book ISBN: 978-93-87456-93-8
E-Book ISBN: 978-93-87456-94-5

Zorba Books Pvt. Ltd.(opc)
Gurgaon, INDIA

Printed at Repro Knowledgecast Limited, Thane

"I ACKNOWLEDGE WITH GREAT RESPECT MY PARENTS, FOR HAVING GIVEN BIRTH TO ME IN THIS GREAT COUNTRY INDIA WHICH HAS NURTURED AND BLESSED ME WITH MUCH KNOWLEDGE"

CONTENTS

PREFACE

The modern world has entered to into a new millennium but from the dawn of civilization till date woman froma patriarchal society, particularly in India, continues to be molested and ill-treated. She is made dependent, weak and is exploited and caused to face gender discrimination in every sphere of life. The gender-based violence that is threatening the wellbeing and dignity and rights of women, extends across the social, cultural economic and regional boundaries. In our ancient mythological text, a woman is considered as Tridevi, as detailed below both in the analysis and her Image. The term Tridevi, the three goddesses in Sanskrit is a concept In Hinduism. Joining *TRIAD* of eminent goddesses whether as genuine version of Trimurthy consists of masculine, depending on the denomination. This triad is typically personified by the Hindu goddesses: Lakshmi; Saraswathi and Parvathi in Shaktiism theory.

Three Trione goddess are the manifestations of Dev, the Supreme Divinity. In the Navarathri (nine nights) Festival "the goddess Parvathi is worshipped for three nights, then Lakshmi on the fourth, fifth and sixth nights and finally Saraswathi until the ninth night. Where as androcentric denominations of Hinduism the feminine Goddess are regarded as consorts and auxiliary deities to the more eminent masculine Trimurthy gods Vishnu, Brahma and Ishwar respectively The Shakti Dharma denomination in the feminine Tridevi goddess are given the eminentroles of creator (Mahal Saraswathi), Preserver (Mahalakshmi) and Destroyer (MahaKali) with the Masculine Trimurthy gods being relegated as the auxiliary deities of the feminine Tridevi.

Instances of violence against women in ancient India are mentioned in Mahabharata where in it was mentioned that the violence was meted to Draupadi. Dharmaraju himself who involved in staking his (their) wife Draupadi in gambling and lost her following which Duryodhana, younger foster brother to Dharmaraju, ordered his brother Dussasana to strip her in the royal court. In Ramayana too, Rama abuses his wife Sita who is incarnation of Lakshmi who commits self-immolation to prove her chastity and on another occasion she was asked to go and live in the forest even after knowing well that is pregnant just on the allegation prompted by a washer man "she is unclean; spoiled"

Though Indian society has always *revered-women* particularly in Hinduism which believes that men and women represent the two halves of a Divine Body. There was no question of superiority or inferiority between man and woman. Hindu history is witness to super women such as Gargi, Maitreyi, Subhadra, Rukmini, Anasuya, Savitri and so many among others whose faculty of reasoning was far superior to that of an ordinary mortal. Many female deities like Saraswathi, Lakshmi and Matha Durga, as analyzed above, are being worshipped across by Hindus in the country since ancient times.

According Mahabharata by cherishing women one who is virtually the goddess of prosperity and wealth.However on the darker side the patriarchal system has continued since the time of Rig-Veda.

Customs and values were made by men to favor men, and women to suffer this discrimination in silence.

Historically, Indian women have been made to adopt contradictory roles. The strength of women is evoked to ensure that women effectively play their traditional roles of nurturance as daughter, mother, sister, wife and mother-in-law. On the other hand stereotype of weak and helpless women is fostered to ensure complete dependence on the male sex.

The following play discusses such events of aggression and violent rapes over the three teen aged girls by their close associates. The play is depicted with full narrations duly inspired by true incidents that took shape that stirred the social life of entire Northerncentral India.

SCENE 1

WHO IS WHY, WHEN AND HOW?

Ramanujam is an Ayurvedic Physician. He could go through the old Ayurvedic books preserved by his ancestors. From those books he could learn how to prepare the medicated powders for the treatment of specific ailments. He also learned from the stored books that the herbs, and plants and products are the portion of metereia medica or in Sanskrit Sushrutha Samhitha Volume I of the Vedic healers. This became his graduation and acquired the decree of Ayurvedic Vaidya Vidhana by himself since he became well versed with language of Telugu and Sanskrit. Plants and herbs are available in plenty in and around the forests whichis nearer to his native village. In those books it was scripted the importance of the Plant which is the major arsenal to combat the human ailments. Thus the school going boy turned as self-made physician of that area.

If we peep in his personal life one can know that, he married an orthodox Brahmin family girl called Saraswathi who later became most suited wife for he never expected should be so cooperative both in personal activity and domestic realm. She handles cooking with all the knowledge of chef. Her simplicity and orthodox way life superseded his style of life. Any way she proved a most qualified wife as described in Neeti Sara of **Manu smruthi** which include:

> *Katveshu Dasi, Karmeshu Mantri Bhojeshu*
>
> *Matha, Shayaneshu Rambha Roopeshu*
>
> *Lakshmi, Kshameshyu Dharitri Shatdharma*
>
> *yukta Kula dharma Patni*

In the village of Dhavaleshwaram, where Ramanujam lives, looks like small helmet on the river banks of Godavari where the river ends and gets amalgamated with Bay Bengal. It is noted sacred place for Hindu's where River Vasishta interlace with his sister Godavari and there is a small temple is called Narasimha Swamy where all devotees offer their prayers. In toto that area called as Anthavedi where goddess Godavari alienate with Purusha Ocean called Bay of Bengal.

Ramanujam built a four bedded house with penthouse on the top. When we enter it looks like Noble king's palace, built in orthodox architecture. In the first year of his marriage, he was blessed with a son and who is called as Satyanarayana. As a matter of fact, Ramanujam is fond of female child.

He expected the same for the next delivery but it could not materialize. It seems she developed with agynecological problem for which he started giving some herbal mixture and later for which it took around 8 years to conceive and deliver three daughters consecutively within three years. Thus his ambition fulfilled. He nurtured them with great enthusiasm and used to supplement them with tonics and syrups to look fair and healthy.

All the three daughters were named as Lakshmi, Saraswathi and Durga being the symbols of Tridevi who are the consorts of Gods, Vishnu, Brahma and Ishwar.

To commemorate the colloquial saying that "Daughters bring wealth and prosperity, his clinic became one of the major Hospitals (Ayurvedic) in that Kona seema and with the result number of patients both from far east central western parts of India used to visit for consultation and treatment. His revenue crossed around one million per year and free supply of grains and pulses by the local land lords whenever the crops gets ready for harvest. This brought riches and since then he became prosperous and wealthy person that counted him elevated tojoin in the elite club of the District. Even after the in-computable wealth, his attitude, simple way of living both by himself and his family and children lead simple life with any royal pinch. One seven Seater car Toyota Innova purchased to meet the needs of frequent travels to district headquarter Rajahmundry for attending conferences, functions and marriages. He along with his family are living happily without any adverse effects Thus he is called as Ramanujam Doctor in that area.

Around 15 years passed. His son became a Post-Graduate and got selection as Probation Officer in a prestigious Scheduled Bank called State bank of India. Ramanujam felt that it is right time to procure suitable bride to suit his sentiments and ambitions. His daughters are also studying well in their academic career. Lakshmi is studying 10th class, Saraswathi 9th class and Durga in 8thclass in the school located in Dhavaleshwaram. Their beauty looked awesome who ever come across them. That is, they are so beautiful and look like Princes. Ramanujam used to be proud of them whenever he looks them that angels have taken birth in his family.

Ramanujam after consultation with his son, invited Sri Nageswara Rao Panthulu (who is also called Pellilla Perayya of that area) to look after a better alliance. He picked up few Bio-data profiles along with Photos. On verification of all profiles that stopped at one point that relates to the daughter of Asst. Divisional Engineer in Irrigation department, who is named after asKoteeswara Rao. The name of the bride is Radhika.

There is one more family in the Dhavalesh-waram, which is friendly related to Ramanujam doctor Garu. And that family belongs to Sri Ramanna Choudhry, and he belongs Kamma community. He is a man of business, moneylender, Contractor and no work is left which fetches money. He has got two sons, better to call them as Rowdy sheeters. While their father is earning millions one side by squeezing poor farmers these two sons are burning his exchequer on alcohol, prostitution on all Underground business like flesh trade, Narcotic supply to the innocent college students. They can be called as spoiled rogues, the children of fat cats. They always stay in Rajahmundry in three star hotels used to enjoy to its pitch by female fiancées around them and sprinkle currency which is not yet demonetized life.

Finally with regard the female children of Ramanujam, we need to tell much squarely. They are so gentle that more fare equal to their fairness. They possess such a beauty and good looking physiognomy that there is no comparison with anybody. No one can make them feel inferior without their consent.

There is another personality who is ex-ceptionally platonic that nobody in India can dare enough to question his Philanthropy. What is that philanthropy let us know later.

District Collector sent an Invitation all the VIP's of village to attend the facilitating meeting being conducted tomorrow 5"O" clock pm. A big and large Open Hall is seems to have booked to facilitate him. The conference Hall is decorated as per the instructions of the District Magistrate that is Collector. Such an embellishment arrangement was prepared that it is meant that some Prime Minister or President of India is going to attend for the recompense?

However all the villagers thought that by evening 5 pm it would be disclosed and hence they did not show much craze? The moment they went through in gathered march lead by Ramanujam to the reception spot', they found embezzled that only 'District collector is presiding the conference'. Any way, they thought, having come to that extent why can't they head for a while so that they can go back to their urgent domestic work to be attended to early. But they noticed later the local MP and MLA are made their way to attend the conference. They puzzled once again what would be the subject matter that is going to be discussed amongst so much hue and cry?

Firstly, the Member Parliament stoodand sited

importance of the gathering that "Mr. Venkateswara Rao son of Anjaiah has created history by discarding the clause from his being Reserved Candidate from the list of *"According Government Jobs in Reserved Category"* and tendered an *affidavit* to the extent that hewould be selected for the jobs only on the *Merit basis* and not from Scheduled Caste Reserved Category. For this "Our District Collector" after channeling and consulting entire Indian States about a candidate, if any, has taken such a daring step in entire India and he is awarding a certificate of appreciation by the Government of Indiathat" being a Scheduled Caste Candidate he, Mr. Venkateswara Rao son of Anjaiah, Resident of Dhavaleshwaram, East Godavari District, Andhra Pradesh has rejected to captivate any job *Reserved* candidate during life time and this decision is an historical event in the Indian History. Thus I on behalf of the Government of India Granting a *title to him as an Man who created History in the History of India. He is a Hero of India"*

On hearing this entire gathering of the spectators who have attended felt proud of his sacrifice and some body went to touch his feet. But Mr. Rao said I am a small man hence do not elevate me to that height. I am proud of my being an Indian which gave me this muchof courage to sacrifice the Reservation and also request my colleagues to disown this type heinous Reservation since I believe that all Men are equal. There would not be Varna system in India as a Country. As long as we feel that "one belongs to that cast this cast, it would lead to Racism and then we fail to practice patriotism with our Nation-Jai Hind"

On hearing his speech everyone who are present felt proud of their village since it be would called a village that has created an Example in entire India. Some students raised their voice and said "Hats Off to Mr. Venkateswara Rao". Miss Lakshmi first daughter of Ramanujam also shouted in rousing slogan "You're Mr. Pride of India" Thus the assembly got disbursed after getting distributed with sweet and savory pockets for every one that has presented there. Thus small miniature family of Anjaiah became a quintessential family of entire district. Anjaiah is a cobbler by caste. Mr. Venkateswara Rao described this event as a small step that upswing to measure Himalayan height.

Ramanujam felt edgy the moment he noticed that a boy from miniature and downtrodden family won accreditation from the political level to village level. Somehow he could not digest the reception given to a low caste person.

But his daughter felt flamboyant the situation. She said to herself' Yes such revolutionary mortal should be extoled so that other should learn his daring step. Such valiant persons and gallantry persons are required to launder the society then only dirt will be cleared.He is a lesson to others, otherwise our society is going on habitude with age old traditions. I want all people to Indian first, Indians last and nothing but Indian. One should feel pride that India has sent to West, such gifts like grammar, logic, Philosophy and fables, hypnotism and decimal system. Our India is so great that nothing has left undone either by man or nature to make most extraordinary country that the Sun visits on his rounds, nothing seems to have forgotten, nothing over looked."

While saying above, she lost herself in the realm of Love, a sweet world where she was flying like a jubilant angel in the arms of Hero Cupid, who looks cute and perfect being and perfect being is none other than Venkateswara Rao. He became such a hero that is what her heart needs all the time. He became a lover at first sight. He became a thing of beauty that gives joy forever.

Ramanujam along with her three daughters left the function Hall and moved back to his venue back. Saraswathi invited them and posed number questions about the function. Ramanujam lightly said some low caste fellow was felicitated with reward as if he reached to Everest peak. It must be the political gimmick to gain votes from low cast communities.

Then Lakshmi interfered and said "What dad? You have simply made that boy as a scapegoat of politics. No never. It is not so. The step he has taken must be unparalleled one in the history of Scheduled caste life. No student in the India would sacrifice his Deserved Reservation. He is most laudable and pride of our area. In the days of malpracticing and misusing government after being obtained false reservation certificates secured from MRO's, Superior Officers in Revenue department by paying hugemoney and using foul ways to get jobs in Government Departments. Hence in my view the sacrifice hemadeneed appreciation."

Saraswathi said "what my dear what is the matter you are bursting out whiling favoring that boy. After all he is a low caste fellow by birth and whatever does need to be deplored and condemned. We are hailing from great forward caste. The knowledge we have is unquestionable and unchallengeable. We are direct descendants of Brahma and so we are the sacred community. Do you understand? We have born direct from the mouth of Brahma, you know. This is clearly authored in Rig Veda"

Lakshmi said" Dear Mom you are really innocent and not aware of the how the knowledge of Universe developed. You must have seen only Radio or Tape recorded while you married and no after 25 years you entire system has changed and the images and voices from our Village will instantly can be witnessed and heard instantly in America which is 12 thousand Kilometers, even those images can travel and can be seen on moon which around 3.5 lakh Kilometers. We have got SMS, Cellphones, smart phones, iPhone, which are the media to connect the entire Globe. Such is the period in which we are running through. In such augmented period. Now you are counselling 5 Millenneium old theories."

In reply Saraswathi said "Oh what a development you have. But eveninthis socalled modern period Sun rising in the East and Sets in the West. Moon'sauscultation has not changed; the number of 24 hours a day and night has not changed, both Sun and Moon's evolution has not changed, timely change of seasons have also not changed; man's appetite, man's timely growth from birth to death has not changed; when you sow seeds of Mango you get Mangoes only from Mangoes and not Potato, you sow Paddy seeds you harvest Rice all and this phenomenon also has not changed. These basic and fundamental process have not changed. In spite these facts that are continued since the formation of Universe without taking shape. This are the Dharma or duties assigned by the God. But you are talkingabout the change?

Yes one thing can be staunchly said that there

is progress of Science since it has discovered and invented so many electronic articles; machines, that could have evolved out of the material available on earth. Machines only reduces our labor not our manual labor. Non-practicing such use of manual labor is causing so many novel diseases like Cancer, Diabetes BP etc. In accordance with these changes the tradition and cultures are being changed which are not related to God but human's trial error practice. In we had bullock carts, Horse carts now Buses, trucks and cars and scooters have come. It is the due to the evolution of knowledge which changed the requirements that changed the style of life both to save time and space and this change stripped the orthodox methods and invented modern methods That is it. However, the basic change that connotes basic infrastructure provided by Mother Nature will never bechanged."

On hearing her mother's spellbound lecture Lakshmi said herself that our mother though looks like orthodox Brahmin but she has enormous knowledge which cannot be countered. Ramanujam also felt strange for her lengthy lecture and felt satisfied that she too possessed with Logical knowledge,

Today being the holiday on account of Independence Day, Lakshmi felt it is necessary to meet Venkateswara Rao. Her heart is always lingering to meet Mr. Rao. Hence started to move out of the house and meet him anywhere near the School. Luckily she could notice him at Tea stall nearby her school. Mr. V. Rao also looking for her ever since he heard a slogan calling me"Mr. Pride of India" he became restless and desired to meet her as early as possible. On seeing her he said in himself that "Oh God you have heard my heart beats" But No God, if he do exists, failed to give any reply either negatively or positively.

However both of them instantly started wishing each other by saying "Hello Sir Mr. Venkat how do you do?"

He in turnsaid "Hello Miss Sri Lakshmi. How do you do"

She with much surprise said" why Shri before name-that is Sri Lakshmi? I am younger than you so no need to use the word of reverence before my name. Moreover that word is used to elderly master or uncles if any. Am I looking older? Is that you?"

"Oh No! I used the word I used was gives different meaning in Sanskrit?" Said Venkat.

She responded immediately by saying "What would be the meaning of that word other than respect?

"Miss Lakshmi, this word connotes Siri and siri means wealth, prosperity, and likewise each God is tagged with this word Sri before their name for example Sri Mahavishnu, Srimannarayana, Sri Brahma, and Sri Nataraja. You know. I thought you know better than me since you have the knowledge of Brahma. Is it not?" retorted Venkat.

"Okay. Leave that matter. I have seen you here on my way hence I wished you, Guruvugaru!"

"Please stop elevating me to the level of Teacher, Miss?" Said Venkat.

Venkat offered her seat and ordered to the boy to supply "two cups of strong tea"

She said No Mastaru thanks for the offer. Generally I don't take in the afternoon time"

Venkat said"don't feel shy be informal. It is only tea wherein milk tea powder and milk along with sugar is mixed and boiled that's all hence no problem please"

"Of course" she took it for drinking and put the cup on the plate meant for it but her position looks nervous as many people who are passing by may attract their attention and they start twittering this news as viral and if this information may reach to her parents it is so because her parents are not that moderate to allow her daughter to meet some strange person outside her house.

Venkat could understand her position and hence he asked her to go near the school and "sit in the parking place"

She immediately accepted his offer and said Okay Guru" Both of them moved away to the parking place and had chit chat for about an hour. During their chit chats their expressed "their inner voice of Love". Both said each other to wait for the right time since her brother's marriage is taking place in this week end. Then they decided to get disbursed and moved to their respective houses.

But for our surprise, a man who is almost middle aged one has started taking video and audio since he seems to be a professional informer. The moment they started meeting each other and disbursed at the end, bit by bit video and audio recorded and at the end it seems he has aired through a watsap or SMS the person who has hired him. We do not know to whom he is working and why and what for? Let us know in the consecutive sections. But he took all these live photos somehow by hiding behind the compound of the School Building.

SCENE 2

HAPPY MOMENTS OF TRIOS FAMILY

All most all the comrades of Family including Seetha Ram took Toyota Innova and moved to Rajahmundry to the celebrate of the marriage of Seetha Ram, on Sunday morning as it was day of Dasami which is considered an auspicious day, in Hindu tradition. Sri. Koteeswara Rao, being a Divisional Engineer in Irrigation Department has minted anomalous wealth (black money) that made him to sprinkle huge sums on the occasion of marriage function.

Nearly 3000 invitees were present andvarieties of dishes both in Non-veg and Vegetarian were prepared and served. He gave 25 acre wet land along with cash around another 25 lakh in the name of dowry plus gold, and dresses as if it is being given to the bride to wear them for her entire life span. The dresses include popular and prestigious Banaras, Dharmavaaraam and Mysore Silk sarees costing to the extent of around 20 to 30 thousand each. At same time he received costly tributes by way of gifts from the invitees.

For a normal spectator, it appears as if he is

running Marriage business in which the more you invest the more you get profits. The revenue that he collected through gifts, became bounteous than his investments. Likewise the black money becomes laundered through such functions.But when we see economic graph, India stood 15th poorest economy in the world! Alas! Let the God save our country. Marriage is over and nuptial too completed and all hosts and guests moved back to their respective houses.

All most 5o million transaction took place, but still no one felt the affliction, but found happy. But unfortunately some mourning occasion appeared on the stage. It so happened that the bride party is about to hand over the bride in the hands of groom for future responsibility. While departing the bride, all most all the female relatives and parents started weeping to place her palms in the palms of the groom. Then the groom started worrying why all the bride side people are weeping? He questioned all the attendants what is that happened that made you weep so grievously.

Then Saraswathi said," nothing happened, it is only a formality to weep and feel grief while bidding farewell their daughter".

Another lady from brides' camp started saying in moaning face "see Mr. Groom Seetha Ram, the bride was given with much affection and love that she did walked on the floweryflooring and she did not put her feet on the floor. That was how she nourished in this house for the past 20 years and such girl we are departing todayand handing over to you so that you ought to look after her well for the rest of the life"

Then Groom started crying loudly. The mother of the bride asked him "why my son-in-law you are crying so seriously".

For that He replied "O mother–in-law, you are all crying for departing her just after nourishing her for 20 years only, then what would be my position when I have to nourish her for 80 years and that is the reason am crying dear mother -in-law Garu".

On learning this all the attendants laughed in high pitch for cutting the joke suitable to the occasion and the happy scenario glittered further. But our heroin Miss. Lakshmi is in different mood, and thinking of Mr. Venkat all the while.

Ramanujam suddenly came there and said" why you are standing here in seclusion. All of our party members are there at the "departing of Bride" ceremony, what is the matter my princes? Why you are moody? Please tell me.

She Said "No Dad I am alright I am Okay fine. See I am coming."Finally they took the bride along them and driven to Dhavaleshwaram. One small but serious incidents took place in between the ceremonies of marriage. Lakshmi, Saraswathi and Durga both trios went around the house and comparing their house with bride's house. It is a normal process of feeling jealousy among the woman folk of the bride and grooms families. Hence they started weighing the affluence among the groom and bride parents wealth. On survey the trio noticed bride's side house is more luxurious than theirs at village comparatively.Meanwhile some young guy not yet introduced with them attempted to take rounds of them with glittering eyes.

He asked "Miss Lakshmi are you all related to Groom's Group. If so how much you are related to the Group, because you look so beautiful that only Tridevi' that they roam in heaven"

But Lakshmi bluntly replied and said "Who the hell you are. How dare to grade our beauty. We are beautiful or not what matters you to comment?"

He, to their dismay, said that "I am a brother of the bride Radhikaand my father is Koteeswara Rao D.E. Is it enough? I am Chiranjeevi by name and I am in final year Engineering."

Then all of three simultaneously cut a sorry face and said "We are sorry. We are the younger sisters of the Groom, Mr. Seetha Ram, and Manager of SBI

Branch at Eluru, and our eponyms Lakshmi, Saraswathi and Durga. Do you know?"

"Oh God! Then we are relatives by and large. Please accept revered prayer O Devi's. Okay then let me call our house boy to bring strong and hot Horlicks to drink so that your glamour looks more alluring?"

All the Trios said in one tone that "No. We all had coffee just now. Thanks "and they do not have further words to speak and hence started to move away.

Then instantly like a bolt from blue, he asked to stop and said with much speed like a bullet from gun that "But I have fallen inlove with you all, but cannot marry all of you Miss Beauties. Hence, please tell me the name to whom can I marry since we are all tied with close relationship. Please spell out with whom I can marry?"

All of the trios felt uneasy and shy in responding to his questions. Any how they simply escaped and ran away from the spot.

Chiranjeevi felt excited after their serial beauties. All are equally look fair, beautiful, pretty and gorgeous. Words are being fallen short to describe their beauties. What all the terms of beauty he knows he has illustrated..

He became so fidgeted that he wanted to contact his father immediately without wasting time. So moved like a bullet and catch hold of his parents and started interrogating with anxiously his father "to arrange to tender marriage proposal to one of the sisters of his brother-in-law Seetha Ram, as all his sisters are equally look gorgeous." His father said him " Please cool down first and later exhibit your cause of anxiety"

Chiranjeevi turned aside and told his mother also that " See Mummy, Dad is taking lightly to my words please advise him"

"Yes My dear prince cool down first." And by saying it she gave a glass of water to drink to cool him. She again said "This boy is always behave like that whenever he experiences of the strange occasions"

Koteeswara Rao told him "See my boy. There is much time to decide such things. You know that your sister has just married and went to her destiny. You are in such a stage that you have to complete your graduation and then domicile a job for you for settlement and then we can go for alliance. You take the example of your brother in law, he did his studies completed and fetched the suitable job and finally he got prepared for the marriage. That is the process of time factor. He said further you better concentrate on studies and trials for soliciting the job then we can go them and demand for the alliance that is it!"

Mr. Chiranjeevi felt disappointed after having learned all these procedures, got disappointed and moved away to his room for rest. However he is still pondering the alliance to set soon. Thus the chapter of "Happiness is an occasional episode" can be drawn with a border line.

SCENE 3

SERIES OF MOLESTATIONS

Miss Lakshmi the beauty of the family is always thinking of Mr. Venkat. In her view he is so smart and unique personality to reckon with in entire India who though belongs to low caste he behaves as polished and classy as possible. He can be termed as rolled model of "The Man of perfection".

He proved himself as revolutionary and exemplary personality she has ever seen either in History or recent past. He is truly Ideal personality one should be admired and award him with the title of Exemplary Personality of Andhra Pradesh or for that matter entire India. Now her position became bizarre that she is unable to control herself in spending further split of a second that she rushed up from the house tocuspidate with Mr. Venkat.

The position of Mr. Venkat also became analogous and he too rushed out from the house to propitiate with her fiancée. Both met at the Tea stall and wanted to lean on each other and hug each other, but the decorum prevented. Of course they both wished each other and they were forced to go back to their pavilion. Their position became worse than Romeo and Juliet. Lakshmi went back to her bedroom with full of tears in her eyes.

Her body is unable head the ethics. She became so rousing sexually that she embraced the pillows so tightly that she forgot the world and started dreaming that she is in cupid arms. All of a sudden her mother and wake her up to drink the milk. All of sudden she took the glass and drank the entire milk at a stroke and went to the deep sleep. After an hour somebody came to her bed and shook her for split of a second and noticed that she is in the pensive state.

This thug removed her bracelets and liners of the inner part and embraced and her totally and started fucking conjoined with fore play. The moment his body touched her naked body, she through her misty mood also cooperated in the same way as that fellow did. She felt in her heart that it must be Mr. Venkat who utilized her for the entire night twice or thrice like a Bonobo and made her entire body wetted with semen saliva, and finally penetrated his entire weapon in side her vagina and removed itand sprinkled out his semen on the upper side of the whole vagina for third time. It appears that he would have taken some drugs which enables a person to do sex for three or four times within hours. As she is in flying in fairy world, she never or for that matter hesitate to open her eyes as shebecame so drowsy as if she is drowned and drenched in barrelful liquor as it is a primary and inaugural sex experience. The moment he sprinkled his honey in her pussy, all of a sudden liquid from vagina also came like flood of Godavari.

It was most thrilling experience for her as he has inaugurated the opening ceremony of her vagina by scissoring vaginal ribbon.Her body did not respond to wake up in the morning and hence she slept till sun gave warning that it was 11. 0'clock. Even then she continued to sleep.

Saraswathi, came to Lakshmi's room shouted like 1000 Amp blower, and said "what is this Lakshmi don't you know how much day has passed? The times now is half past 11. Don't you go to school? Come on get up and become fresh."

Lakshmi is still in that fairy world, she is unable to get up and come to her senses. But with great difficulty she got up from the bed and straight away entered in to Bathroom. She bolted the Bathroom door and looked her body position. The moment she saw the patches of dried thick liquid, she became thunder struck. How is that all this patches on her body particularly around her inner valley? She questioned herself that "dreams are related to her impulsive mode of thoughts, but all these patches are physically maneuvered? How is that? She also noticed some red dots near her vagina? Oh God! Did

Venkat really came and penetrated me?

She started recollecting the events that occurred in the night in a sequel order (i) first entered bed room with great exiting mood after meeting Mr. Venkat (ii) secondly I took lunch by 2 O'clock (iii) thirdly, laid down on the bed for a while (iv) Then after an hour so I took coffee and started going throughthe News Paper (v) fifthly I again went to see Venkat. I saw him and had a date in the park for a while (VI) sixthly I came back with the un-quenching thoughts and lie down on the bed. (vii) Seventhly Mummy called me attend for the dinner at 8 'O'clock (viii) eighthly I took dinner with two chapattis'and potato curry (ix) Ninthly I went for walking withinthe premises of our compound And tenth and I went to bed"

Our teacher once told me for keeping health one should follow the formula which runs like this "After lunch rest a while (Siesta) and after supper walk a mile" hence I adopted this formula started doing continuously since two years. Finally her mother came to "my room and gave routine **Glass of Milk** finally I went to bed to sleep. But I don't know why I got spell-casting sleep immediately after laying on bed. That is all. Nowhere have I come across with Venkat physically except in dreams.It that is the case How come this gum type patches on my body. I have also experienced a deep penetration of rod like thing in my body while dreaming.

On analyzing these events she came to conclusion which speaks that: *"I was used for intercourse without my consent and that is improbably a Rape-She* was raped by somebody not known to her. How one new person can enter in her house? If at all he attempted for entering the house, he has to come through main door which is always shut and locked with bothbolts and Lock during the night hours.

However while taking bath, she thought it is better to contact Mr. Venkat immediately after breakfast. After eating Idli-vada with coconut chutney, she moved out without hesitation and go on searching him on the pass road and also near School and the park nearby school. But he found nowhere and she moved to his house directly and on an enquiry with his mother she noticed that Mr. Venkat has left already in yesterday morning to report to the job in Gandhi College of Commerce at Rajahmundry. Another shocking news! She questioned herself why did not he inform her about his job? Why? Immediately she moved to Bus stand and catch the Bus to Rajahmundry and contacted the Principal of the college.

He said "we gave a call on yesterday morning about 10.30 he then appeared here about 12 noon and gave a joining report immediately and he attended the class. On learning from the students that the new lecturer is a brilliant man and possessed with full of vast knowledge in fields including current affairs. While she was returning to her village to attend the school, Venkat appeared before her. He said "What a surprise! Oh my god. Come on in our staff room and discuss the matter. He asked her what made you to come to me so fast. Whether there is an exigency in your house about your marriage?"

She said "no nothing. But some untoward incident has happened about which I would like to tell in seclusion."

"Okay" said Venkat to wait here with any objection from our staff members. I will be back within an hour."

She took the chair and started silently crying for the last night's incident which is hunting her since she woke in up in the morning. Tears shedding like waterfall, from eyes. She feared about the informing her rape case to others including Venkat and hence she slipped out to bus stand and catch her bus and went to her class room to hear texts of chemistry lesson.

Just an hour later Venkat came saw her in staffroom, but she is not there, then he searched in entire nearby area. He tried to contact her through his mobile phone, but the failed to attend since the phone is switched off mode.

Next day in an early hours that Chiranjee-vi, brother her sister-in- law arrived to whom Ramanujam and his wife received with warm welcome.

He started looking those Trios, but no body found seen. However Ramanjam's second daughter has just arrived from the Tutorials or so and on seeing him she became jubilant and wished him and went the kitchen brought a cup of coffee and gave to him. He enquired about the welfare of all the Trios and got convinced that they may also be present there shortly. However to his surprise, they also made their entry immediately and they started enquiring about their brother and sister-in-law. He promptly said that "I too don't have any idea about them who are at Eluru West Godavari district which is the West Side River Godavari. Lakshmi asked Saraswathi that " have you not looked after well to our Bava garu (brother in law)"

Then suddenly Chiranjeevi said " Oh no not like that , she has just give a Switzerland coffee and I just now drank it"

"Is it so said Saraswathi?" said Lakshmi"

"No. I am sorry I have bluffed you. I have taken a volcanized Coffee for your information please?

Then Okay Lakshmi told him in reply while in

smile. She and Durga sent inside their leaving Saraswathi alone before him, for him they felt she is the suitable girl to tackle him both in relation and joke Chiranjeevi felt it is right thing they both have done as he is very much fond of her. He felt she would be suitable tohim and to his family and besides this she is at present minor and by the time he complete his degree and settle in any job, she cannot be given to marriage until and unless he settle down.

All of a sudden the main door was pushed in side from outside by Ramanujam with slang. He looked furious that "the guest must be Mr. Venkat. How dare he entered my house without prior permission? I will see his end"

Chiranjeevi felt trembled on seeing in his wild face.

Then Ramanujam on seeing his face he cooled down and he wished him "Oh. You. I am sorry I didn't know that it is you. Sorry. Be seated and I will come with a cup of coffee"

"No Mastaru I had it just now. Aunt has just now sent both water and coffee through sister-in-law." "Oh No. Saraswathi, see who has come! You prepare Guttivankaya Kura, Pulihora, Curd and Payasam in the lunch" ordered Ramanujam"Oh No uncle, I have to go to city as sister and brother-in-law are arriving by lunch time, so I have to go there to attend them."

Ramanjam's second daughter whose is name is also Saraswathi is hiding behind bedroom door and heard the entire discussion. Her heart is sending message to Chiranjeevi to stay till lunch as advised by her father. Her hiding behind the door is also being observed by Chiranjeevi and his heart also supporting to stay here for some more time.

But etiquette came in between their slang expressions. He understood that uncle is in serious mood who seems to be against such hide and seek business hence he took decision and moved outside and fared good bye to all and took an auto and left to the city. Before leaving, he signaled as a reply to her signal of love puff and she also received and smiled gently with great anxiety.

She approached Lakshmi informed how she got fascinated by him. Lakshmi said with frustration mood, that "Please do not fall in romance with anybody you need pay much torment in this house as I….. (She stopped) and said better wait until marriage as long as you stay in this house." She intentionally avoided to let her know her worst condition of victimization of rape that took place two days before and suddenly she went to her bed room and started crying by taking pillow in her hand. She is unable to wipe out those spoliation scenes.

Saraswathi took her sisters behavior as strange.

She thought this wouldn't not be the right occasion to enquire about the cause of agony. All of them took lunch in the noon and lie for a while in their respective bed rooms. Durga also simulate the suit and took rest on the bed for a while. She also thought why her both elder sisters' are serious and in a perverse mood. She also felt melancholic since the arrival and abrupt departure of the brother- in-law Chiranjeevi.

Entire day gone passed in routine activities and in the night each of them went to sleep after them performing some post supper exercise of walking.

But Saraswathis position became different. Mr. Chiranjeevi has clocked up her thoughts. His lovely and manly facet has charmed her totally and made her feel intrigued. Suddenly their mother called all of them to take "glass of milk and sleep in dreams" She said good night and left the scene.

But Saraswathis' thoughts are being hunted by Chiranjeevi, his face his manliness, cute personality she said suddenly "Ow" and then kept silent. "But waves of romancing engulfed her moods and she went drenched in the nectar of love and fell in-depth sleep. Suddenly the image of Chiranjeevi' is, screened in the theatre of her mind and he joined her for singing duot like male and female angels in the fairy surfing clouds.

She felt that he came over and occupied her entire body and peeled the pieces of gown and her inner and made naked and also threw his dress too totally and she became layer of his body, his kisses on the petal lips, cream piles dulypuffed innumerable times, his hard rock palms touched the silky petal in between her gammons, and started penetrating his cock that she never knew, was started playing dim and dip games by putting and withdrawing for an innumerable times, turned her reverse and penetrated his cock between the buttocks Oh what an extraordinary experience Oh My god. She said in ecstasy that "You have sent Mr. Chiranjeevi to screw her body with thick diamond rod. Oh what a pleasant thing and he finally drenched her body with a gummy liquid may be semen and it seems he slipped away. She wanted to catch him again but he is no more there. Perhaps he has disappeared from the fairly land." But she could not wake up as she is so drowsy that she is unable to open her eye lids.

But suddenly in the early hours of morning he came again and repeated the same game of dim and dip and poured some more liquid on her nipples and on her sheath and she also emitted liquid.

As there was a holiday, all most all members of her family are still in sluggish mood. Our Junior Saraswathi who wanted to sleep sill, all of a sudden woke up with jolted shock. She noticed that her "entire body became patchy with thick patches in and around the central part of her legs and on nipples of her boobs. How is that? She said herself "I was in dreamy fairly land in sleep but now her body is full of semen patches from her boobs to pussy?" None is seen in the in house except their parents and sisters no other male members are seen in the premises. How can psychological thoughts secrets physical liquid spread on her sensitive areas" Oh, No! She went to bath room. She is unable to identify actual cause for those patches? Her position is in fix, and her thoughts are emitting flurry warm breeze? She doubted that her body is full of squeezes with embracement. Why and how? She doubted "Am I raped by somebody physically? The very thought of rape became embarrassing to her. She noticed some red spots on the bed and finally he has say that is she was brutally raped in her own secured nest? If sowho could he be?"

After taking bath she again started thinking" If at all that Chiranjeevi comes inside the house how can he enter the house? There is only one way left that is main door? She said" I have seen with my senses that he moved out in Auto to catch the bus at bus stand. To confirm his absence in the night she phoned Chiranjeevi and in turn he responded that he is "recollecting you and your beautiful and graceful looks since night" There is no possibility or least scope to enter any body after the door is bolted within from inside?" She started weeping and went to her elder sister to discuss the issue. But she is not in her bed room. She suspected something is mischief is going on in the house. Lakshmi is also gloomy since two days past and for what reason? She don't know. She took breakfast and left the house and the breeze of open air gave some consolation. She took company of her sister Durga and reached near School compound. Incidentally their elder sister is sitting alone is in some gloomy mood!

Both rushed to her and started going on questioning about her inattentive behavior with all the members of family? The moment started enquiring about her dull and gloomy behavior, Lakshmi burst out with much distress and anguish and said" I have lost myself includingmy virginity which has hampered me to go into depression. I am unable explain as to how, somebody came to my chamber and raped bluntly and I am not in a position to name the miscreant" She further continued "my life is over I became a tormented doll now? Some time I felt to commit suicide since no way is seen helpful?I am a spoiled girl and hence there is no way out say that I want to live? Now there is no meaning to life."

On seeing her in such melancholic and depressed life, both the sisters cried since they don't have enough words to sympathize her and there is no use also? It is all   due to the wrong identification of a woman in society which always supports the crimes of Male and not the woman. Women's life in Indian society is like "rose petal falling on the thorn" that is in both ways she becomes a victim of abuse. While criticizing the society they want to know what actually happened and when?

For that Lakshmi narrated the entire story bit by bit since she could not discuss about the matter with her parents.

On hearing this, Miss Saraswathi also cried and said that the same thing has happened during the last night when Mr. Chiranjeevi paid visit. The mystery furthered their anxiety as to" why these things are being happened in our house alone". They started thinking what made them so drowsy when some-one is coming and doing all sorts of dirty work and disappeared form the realm of their house. Who could be that fellow? Is that rascal is from within our family or outsider the family. Lakshmi said "Okay when if such thing has happened due to my negligence, I feel I am wrong from my side since I loved Mr. Venkat and he would have entered house by hook or cook and did all that dirty things. I can point out that fellow to have done such activity? But in your case it is still strange to note that Mr. Chiranjeevi had come and left the house within an hour after taking coffee etc."

But how about the night what made some-body to dare to enter in our house? Does it not look strange? No male person except our father is there in our family? We cannot work out to decide who that outsider is. We cannot point out our finger on Chiranjeevi? Now I have decided to chase that fellow who is coming inside and doing all the business? Let us safeguard our self hereafter!

While coming back to their house, theTrio came across with two bike riders to whom they do not know. Both of them wantonly took their bikes and they gave small hit on Durga and Saraswathi.

Both of them started abusing them as "You fools rascals' scoundrels how you dare hit us"

One among them said "Sorry Miss. See Baby, let me introduce ourselves with you, we are Ajay and Vijay sons of Raamanna Chaudhary, the most noted and influencedpersonality of the village. Do you know? Hello what about you beauties?"

"You shut up. Give way to us first. What if you are sons of Raamanna or Krishnanna? No matter for us. We are children of Ramanujam Panthulu. You know?"

"Oh Doctor is it? We know him. Great man for us all. But we will come to your father for giving either of three for marriage with us. We will be future

MLA of this area you know."

"No matter either you will be MLA or Municipal sweeper; doesn't matter us. You fools. Here no body is waiting to marry you, and this for your kind information Mr. Ajay." Said Lakshmi.

Then Ajay said "Oh Miss. Don't be so arrogant. You hit our vehicle; not we? We had just parked our vehicles here your sister'trio gave dash to our vehicles. Any way I apologize with you all. Okay. We would come to your father and ask your sisters in marriage"

Lakshmi said "Oh No who will marry with such rouge like you and that too you belong to non-Brahmin family where as we hail from forward class in Society. You are Non-vegetarian, eating flesh and blood of animals which is cruel culture thatyou belong?"

Ajay said "Oh. No. This is too much. It is you people got separated from the society and maintain superiority and untouchability with non-Brahmins. This wouldn't be illegal, maintaining racial spirit among humans? We are born equal and hence Human is one, as per the UN Directive Principles, don't you know? Your community caused atrocities and vulgarity that segmented system with other humans. You considered sacred and made us Sudras into 4th class citizens which would be considered as illegal in the present days. You discarded us from entering the Temples, by taking and using water that belongs to your Agraharam community?

This is totally fallacious and red tape system that has been practiced by you people since thousands of years. And the basic contention most of you Brahmins do not know it that "One who has Knowledge of Brahman, he is considered as Brahman hence whoever have that Knowledge he would be called Brahmin, so if I have that Knowledge I may be coined as Brahmin and Brahmins who doesn't have Brahman or Vedic knowledge he cannot be called a Brahmin, the birth from Brahmin family also cannot be called automatically asBrahmin You know Miss better you know?

"How is that it must be your tailor-made theory? Nobody will accept your ascetic preposition. We have been acclaimed as higher class in the society. It is told in Rig-Veda that" who ever take birth from the mouth of Brahma, are termed as Brahman; whoever take birth the shoulders of Brahma are termed as Kshatriyas; Whoever take birth from stomach of Brahma, are termed as Vysya and whoever take birth from the feet of Brahma are called as Sudras. You know. Go and refer Vedas. This knowledge we have from Vedas itself connotes that we are True Brahmans. So you need not and cannot question the Vedas. Mind it, you better mind it"

"If that is the case we came to know that you are in love with Mr. Venkat. Then how is that? What reply you can endowed with? You are a Brahmin and he is a lowest cast, below Sudras? What do you say for this? We are better than those Mlechhas? He was not at created with any part of Brahma? They belong heinous caste. How is that you involved in love affair with those Madiga caste?"

Now Lakshmi's position became cornered. However she became stubborn and said" who said I am in love with him? I appreciated for his daring step to strip his caste when the question of reservation arises. That daring step made me to appreciate him as Man to reckon with. That is why I groove on. That's it. You must know Mr. Ajay, better you know.

"Ajay said "don't bluff me. Entire village know about your affair with that dirty Venkat."

For that statement, she became nervous reddish and ran away from the spot along with her sisters.

Then Ajay shouted by saying "This shows that silence is half-truth and hence you are really in love with that bloody rogue. We are better than him. He is a son of a cobbler and his earning is not sufficient for his family's hand to mouth. You see we are wealthy I think more that you too. Hence convince your father by saying that Ajay and Vijay are offering their readiness to marry your younger sisters' one for me and another to Vijay. Right."Thus they also took their bikes and drive away.

It is however, our CID seems to have taken up his job and aired the entire scenes through whatsap to his boss. Who is that Boss we yet know?

While moving through auto the third sister Durga is in her high spirits. It seems she has fallen in love with Mr. Ajay. She, in heart, started saying that "his analytical and intelligent interpretation of the caste system became a thing of her attraction. She supported his view of human life in general. Yes,what he said is correct while stating that "All humans are equal that draws a conclusion that all humans are one.

She has studied one such article that was published in the News Paper. Since then she formed her opinion on that direction. She also concluded that "our caste system is meaningless". Of course it would have been the profession that could have partitioned the humans in to caste or class system.

She argued herself that "when astudent gets morethan 80% marks in SSC/ or any examination, he is called as a Distinctive person, if one gets 60 and above, we call him First class student, if he get less than 60 and 50 he is called as second class and if one gets just below 50 –to 35 he is called third class student and finally if he gets 35 and below he is termed as failed candidate. But to say reasonably, Sudras or SC and ST mat get more that 60 he is called first class and other forward caste student gets 35 he is called as failed student is it not? That means we humans have compartmentalized ourself on the basis of color and creed, caste, and Race system.

Another argument she designated that by profession one can called as Pujari, carpenter, tailor, cook, weaver or washer man or even cobbler or barber. But all these human beingsareprofessionals in their respective fields and they cannot be termed as low caste people whoare biologically equal. So the classifications and compartmentalization are formed by humans based on their profession and not by birth. Brahmin may do barbers work and Sudra may do Pujari work by learning Sanskrit. There is no another reason for this. Reasoning, intelligence is no man's or no caste's property; everybody can be intelligent and reasoning that does not mean that a person that reasons and argues intelligently belong to certain category of caste or race.

Again regarding fair color Brahmins argue that all most all Brahmins are white and have fair color. But I have seen black colored Brahmins and fair colored Sudras or Mlechhas. Hence what Mr. Ajay said is correct! Another example she desired to spell out is, take the functioning of an Office of any government or NGO, thetop grade Officers, that is, A like IAS/IPS, then Group B Officers, Then Group C officers and finally group D. It is obvious that in these groups there may be Brahmins in low category or Sudras in top category of Group A. That distinction does not mean they belong to these individual castes. Thus Class Caste, Creed, Color belongs to nobody's property. All biologically equal. Brahmin has the same blood as Sudras possess. The entire anatomy of human body has no difference biologically."

While thinking all these events, she forgot to step down from the auto when her other sisters started getting down as their house neared. Lakshmi called Durga" come on get down we have arrived near our house". Then she came into consciousness started stepping down. By the time they entered the house, their brother Mr. Seetha Ram and sister-in-law seen in the drawing room partaking coffee.

All of them went to see him and wished them with warm welcome. They felt is so nice to see them after long time. Each one congratulated for them for having started a wedded life. They enjoyed both and went to sleep to respective bedrooms.

Their father too wishedthem and asked to take rest. While leaving them he said that "we can discuss tomorrow "said Ramanujam and disappeared from there. Saraswathi went to write Ramakoti as usual to complete the one crore names of Ramaand satisfied that she would be nearing to attain salvation (Moksha).

As usual all the three daughters took the milk and sprawled to their respective Bed rooms to sleep since they feel they are tiered with the discussion with that fellow with that rouge Mr. Ajay.

But Durga's condition became distinct since she started loving Mr. Ajay and his profile. While thinking about him she became autohypnosis and went to deep sleep. She started dreaming about Ajay and seems to have fell in love with him due to his analysis about the casteism. Around 12.30 midnight someone entered in the Durga's room started occupying her made her naked and he made self-naked and started pissing and kissing Durga. As she is in dreaming mood she started with dreaming and extended her cooperation with that culprit and this made him to use her as he like. He fucked her with number shots and she took his cock in between her boobs and he took it to her lips and started kissing and sucking since it is that act has raised her to the uncontrollable ecstasy, the boundaries of it she failed to know. While withdrawing his cock he sprinkled his semen on the entire body of the innocent girl who age is around only 15 years.

Thus this fellow, whoever he may be, utilized the young and teenaged and unmarried girls and subjugated them for his squat of lust. He made utilized all the three young and girls and looted their chaste and virginity. That is he must be great personality for having tasted three virgins at a stretch. Even Bonobo cannot do that act in Jungle.

He felt so satisfied that he has witnessed the heaven on the earth itself. Does it not look great? The entire family would be on roads if it comes to the notice of the society and village elders. Let us see what would happen? Future is the answer for all the questions that were raised in present and past. Past his History, present is Gift and future is a mystery. Let us see and wait for the judgment of the Mother Nature, the better consciousness that injected the injection of humanity in all the humans while they took birth. But some humans behave worse than animal though animal after delivering its offshoots, she look after them so affectionately and proved full length shelter till they grow up. There after they forget and feel their own creations as another animal and co mates each other without knowing they are closed related one. It is so because they do not have sufficient knowledge or remembering capacity as man has. So it is considered as natural for doing sex with mother and son or daughter to father. It is all due to their mind set which is limited to action not reasoning. Man also is an animal but he has super brain to think, wish, reasons, feels because he has grown brain infused in his skull by the nature. He has a brain that has equity of weight with that of human forehead, and the nerves multi-circuited that suits to his body function, besides reasoning.

Humans are widely assumed to the most intelligent species on Earth, due to our intricate civilizations and innovative behavior. The enlarged foreheads and skull capacity of humans has enables our brains to grow in size dramatically from that of our ancestors called animals or even called as Mammals. Neo cortex ' anew out layer of brain that controls complex functions such as consciousness, thought language and self-awareness. There are whole host of cognitive abilities which are uniquely HUMAN, that no other animal could either exhibit or contend with. All of the following behaviors as well as many other imaginative concepts have currently been demonstrated exclusively human. (i) Advanced planning (ii) humor (iii) appreciation of morality (iv) Morality or humanity (v) adaptation to unsuitable environments for example deserts and frozen lands (vi) religion and worship (vii) Vulnerability to neuro- psychiatric diseases, (viii) enhanced connection between neurons and (ix) Non personal comprehension and (x) uncivilized and crooked motivations.

The self-awareness distinguishes from most other species. In Psychology, self-awareness is defined as metacognition, awareness of one's own ability to think. In human, metacognition and other advanced cognitive skills such as social-intelligence planning and reason are all thought to depend on the regions of brain called prefrontal cortex.

Ultimately it is not cognizable who is that fellow, that monster, that Bonobo that has looted from the innocent teens both the chaste and Virginity.Is he still in animal stage or Psychic-human?

India has a culture rooted in both its tradition and culture as well as its British colonial legacy, which blames victims of rape, is sympathetic to perpetrators and which treats women have been raped "as damaged goods" or "slipped leg" who then suffer afterwards. While there are laws written in the books to protect victims of rape; there are lawsare often not enforced, especially the perpetrator is from most powerful caste or wealthier than the person who was raped, there is often a failure to properly gather evidence from rape victims and to care for them evidence from rape victims and to care for them after wards and there is little legal assistance for them.It is however a sympathy or rather advises will be delivered but nobody come forward either to marry or daringly provide them socially. Thus the ultimate sufferer is the Victim herself and have lifelong agony. Everybody surmise the victim with erotic core of ideas.

Let us throw light on these three sisters fate as to how they face the further onslaught and how they react with the culprit?

SCENE 4

SERIES OF INTERROGATIONS AND INVESTIGATIONS

Raamanna Chaudhary on one fine morning came to Ramanujam. Ramanujam is busy with the preparation of some Ayurvedic Powders clubbing Herbs and dry petals of most of the flowers. Choudhry wished "good morning Panthulu garu" and in response to his wish, asked to come inside the house. He ordered his assistant who joined very recently in his clinic for grinding and mixing the powders that Ramanujam prepare.

Ramanujam moved from his clinic and went inside the house and opened the main door and he also asked about Choudhury's welfare. He ordered his wife Saraswathi with two cups of tea. She brought the same and after sipping it Chaudhary started asking "Where are your naughty Tri-Goddesses Mr. Ramanujam Garu?"

In reply Ramanujam replied that "they must have gone to school. Then "what is the purpose of your visit, any surety or witness need to be signed for poor loaners. Please tell me" asked Ramanujam.

"No. Not for any such thing; but out of my curiosity I just asked about them because they are your pretty princes. Is it not?

"OH. There is no doubt about that, because I am their beloved father who is a king of this area. Is it not Mr. Chaudhary? I cannot go for clinic before seeing them on the morning hours of Sun Rise. They are my Goddess you know? Said Ramanujam. "I will not go even for taking bath in Godavari without seeing them. This has become my routine activity?" added further.

Chaudhary Said "Right I would be the person exploring you and your family movements and I feel proud for having such family as my nearest neighbors in the village." He further continued that "On that day it seems you gave fine and emancipating lecture on "exterminating the casteism from the India, while praising Mr. Venkat son of a cobbler Anjaiah. Is it not? I became overwhelmed with joy for your arguments"

Ramanujam said "it wasjust to secure the decorum of the assembly. Anyway, why are you recalling that event now? Have you got any Master plan of grabbing that Venkat for the marriage for your only one daughter?"

Choudhry said "No not that because I don't have any daughter for that matter and I do not have cousin daughter too. Even If have had a daughter I would not give to such dirty caste's offshoot. What arewe andwhat arethey? They are miniatures like a crawling creature of the society. I do believe in Casteism as our ancestors have well drafted the society sectionalizing the society in to four fold categories. Though I am a Sudra, I belong to Kshatriya legacy that is Kamma. I would not go for even Kapu Caste which can be termed as lowest caste in the hierarchy of the Casteism."

"I think, you being a Brahmin know well that only Brahmin Vysya and Rajas (Kshatriya) are numerated as high-class castes in the society. This gradation of casteism being practiced since Vedic Period that is around 5000 years back in our sub-Continent. Even in Muslim community there is a gradation of casteism titled as "Syed, Mughal, Pathan and Sheik" when Islam is considered to be a division less community. So my point is we cannot discard our gradation and continue to practice it, irrespective of the some crooks threat or government directives. What do you say? I think I am correct"

He again continued his lecture by saying that" Let us forget all those things, why I have come here is why don't you consider my two sons Ajay and Vijay to marry your either of three daughters."

When Ramanujam started to give reply, but instantly Mr. Choudhury continued to say again that

"Of course I do not ask dowry. But it is up to you to decide to give dowry or not?"

Then Ramanujam started to give reply suitably by saying that "On one side you argue that Casteism need to continued but on the other side you ask your sons for marriage of my daughters who are the children of Vedic Brahmin. Does it not look baffling?

Is it not laughable? You decide first which caste is in top grade and which is second and third? Thus by all means we stand on top and are third grade one so how can you conclude yourself that I would give daughter for the marriage to the third grade caste. Is it matching? Tell me yourself Mr. Choudhry. The answer is in your question itself. Is it not?"

For that Mr. Choudhry got flunked and said "Why I asked for the proposal, just because of your valedictory speech on the reception of Mr. Venkat, which contained total eradication of this Casteism, hence I thought you wouldn't mind in giving your daughter for the marriage of my twins. It is now you have come to true color. I wanted to test you for your way of argument. I came here just to enquire your stand on casteism. So what you gave lecture on thatday was to impress VIPs and Spectators.That means it is also a story of Elephant who has two set of teeth, one to showoff and another to chew with. Is it not?

Ramanujam said "whatever you think of me you think, I am not coming in your way. It is my lookout. Hence you need not interfere with our domestic affair. Okay thank you. I shall take leave" likewise he said and disappeared from the scene.

While going out of the door Mr. Choudhury said bluntly "Let us see what the hell you do?"

Ramanujam shut the door grudgingly moved away to his clinic, since much handful of work is there to attend with.

Ramanujam said in himself that "that fellow Choudhry is posing as if he is gentlemen. Entire district know who that fellow is and what his Sons' are. He is almost a rowdy crook to tell with.

He decided to go Rajahmundry to meet a patient who is bed ridden on account of the trauma of lever malfunction, for that he had given medicine. Hence he decided to give one more of changed medicine further enlarge dose so that he can recover from the chronic ailment.

After giving medicine to the patient at his home he went to see his son and daughter in law at is co-brother's house of Nageswara Rao, DE.

Here in the house of Ramanujam all the three

daughters met in Lakshmi's room and planning to take up the project of Identification of a Culprit who spoiled their future. All the three daughters approached their mother Saraswathi, but she never showed any interest on their plea but she is deeply involved with writing her Ram Koti per day. If that is the project she involved, she cannot attend other works whoever that instigate her.

All the three victims met in Lakshmi's room and started discussing the similarities that took place in their bed room starting from the beginning to the end. They started drawing a sketch and steps by step incidents that took place. They arrived to a conclusionthat all of them had faced similar incidents and experiences. If that is so the culprit should be neither Venkat nor Chiranjeevi and nor even Ajay.

Since when the incident happened they had matching experiences; firstly, the moment we stretched out on the bed we immediately used to get sleep as spontaneous as if it is automatic or instantly like starting the scooter;secondly the moment we go into sleep we started dreaming our respective lovers; thirdly, we promote that sexy and obsessive thoughts and the venture of intercourse take place in dreams itself.

Fourthly, experience the shots, kissing's, emitting of semen and spreading on nipples and in between thighs; fifthly, again after few hours later that fellow come and used to start the business of sex and erotic emitting of his semen both on nipples and in between thighs and gets disappears finally; sixthly' even we strongly desired to open our eye lids and to see him, we failed to do so why? Seventhly, we get up from the bed much later than our usual wakeup from normal sleep other than those specific days. *Eighthly*, we observe with all our senses that the semen patches are actually sprinkled on the specified spots as dreamed in our dreams. *Ninthly*, these similarities directly point out that the entire act was not done physically by some culprit other than our lovers; *tenthly*, and finally that culprit must be either our family member or a person who closely associated with our family. All of trios agreed that it should be a person closely known to us alone, since Venkat, Chiranjeevi or Ajay are not at all close to our family, they cannot know where our bed rooms are, and where our drawing room located?.Then *who could be that bastard?*

Durga said "why not that person Mr. Chalamiah Daddy's Assistant" "He may be culprit is not Lakshmi"

Lakshmi agreed for her logic. But one thing is that young aged boy has joined the duty "as our father's assistant" only three days back, muchlater after our rapping. Any way that could also be possible. Our next step we need to take is fixing cameras in each of our bedrooms based on that we can identify the culprit. Is it not? All of them said "Yes". Lakshmi further said "As this a family matter, we should not disclose this course of action to them, even let him be our father or brother is not it?"

Meanwhile, Saraswathi Jr. raised one more doubt that "In my view it must be an act of the demon who should have grudge against our family" Then all of a sudden Fourthly, we cannot doubt our father since he is looking after with great affection since childhood. Hence we cannot doubt him then who else?"

And pre- finally why could not wake up the moment he touches our body since in normal sleep we being more sentitive female persons immaterially get alerted the moment a male touches on our sensitive part unless he is our husband. But the question is we are yet be married"

And finally how can we go in deep sleep which became more than coma for us not wake up any time during the act. It is why because, we feel uncomforted when we desire to urinate since our unconscious brain called Medulla oblongata will give alarm to wake up and we get up immediately and go to toilet. I have read in my SSC. Perhaps you may not have had come across so far in your biology."

For that Saraswathi said that "I have also read in

my 9th class biological science."

Then all these trio decided that "it was not the act of out sider's act but it must be from inner side of our house only. Perhaps the culprit would have bolted our parents' bedroom and started attempting us. He either have come from up stair or knew the technique to unlock the locked and bolted doors.   It was finally decided to pass the resolution to check the Glass and milk whether in any mixing was made (ii) Let's lock the Upstairs' penthouse so that no one can dare enough to come down and does his job (iii) Let us take up watchman, sorry, watchwomen duty from the night on sequel basis that is one night Lakshmi, another night Saraswathi and third night Durga again repeat the seriatim or say in succeeding basis so that we make sound that gives alarm to the entire house living persons; (iv) We have to install secret and room digital camera which works in dark or bed light focus in each bed room."

They also concluded in the meeting that if we disclose the matter to our father he may make much hue and cry and our chastity would be aired like a virus in the entire village, hence let us not do this at this initial stage and if we fail to identify even after our planned project then we can straight away inform about the happening in the house. "Lakshmi again gave warning other two sisters to watch every move-ment with detective eye.

Next day morning they three started moving to Rajahmundry to purchase CCTV camera. But they informed her mother and father that they are going to school.

While sitting in the bus they started thinking one more truth to known whether rooms are not connected with any electronic piece which is meant for hearing outside near and around their father's clinic.

They landed in the City, purchased cameras along with a detector to identify or to locate spot where electronic gadget is placed in their bed rooms. The cameras are most sophisticated and digitally advanced one which on analysis in forensic lab, we can get brighter image that snapped at first shot. They attended the school for afternoon periods and came back to house after hearing the last bell. After taking coffee of evening session, either of both made themselves stood to watch anybody's entrance and give alarm to Lakshmi who is attending the cameras to fix at unnoticeable spots by anybody other than themselves.

Thus they successfully implanted the Cameras and verified through detector for about any gadgets are available. So entire network is completed.Almost a month passed but these trios could not identify any such symptoms of committing rape.

On observing this lapse, the trios became lethargic and started neglecting to do watching duty during the nights.

Exactly after one month of No Moons day on one fine night the so called Monster started implementing his plan of action of raping. "It seems he has worn mask first attempted raping with Lakshmi with the same velocity and speed for about one hour and skipped away.

Lakshmi could not resist him because of she is in unconscious state without dreams. But this time that fellow did not emit his semen on the body and thighs but emitted straight away in the vagina and tailored the clothes intact, so that victim should fail to note anything.

After two hours he entered the next bedroom and did the same thing with Saraswathi Jr. Similarly after another two hours he entered the next third bed room and repeated the same type of atrocity. Finally he disappeared from the spot. Night passed as usual, Moon failed to visit this night as doesn't want to witness those ghastly events that happened with three trios for the second time. This time that fellow completed his schedule of visit to rape all the three in the same night one after another serially.

Next day morning the trio noticed same type rape as that happened during last month's No-moon day. Again pathetic atmosphere has spread in their life. They started weeping for their aghast fate. They roared and roared for some time, but they have to run the vehicle of life. They felt sorry for the negligence they shown while taking security measures. However one idea made them flashed and that idea was checking the camera fixed in the room.

As a routine affair, they completed their bathroom work and went to kitchen took coffee and started checking the camera screen of each room. For their dismay, the camera snapped the blurred images since there was insufficient light in the room. Beside this the culprit seemed to have wear mask which left confusion to identify them.

But one thing they could underpinned that the physique of the culprit does not tally to any members of family except to that of Ramanujam, their father. However they could not agree to accept the fact that it is their father's atrocities. They cannot think of him in the place of that culprit.

Lakshmi instantaneously suggested them "let us go and check the tumblers through which they were served with the milk in the last night"

They entered the bed rooms but found nothing. They went to see the kitchen where all the used kitchen wear would be placed near wash basin. But learnt that all the items were neatly washed and kept them in their respective places in the kitchen it-self.

All hopes were flattened. The entire project of Detection of the culprit gone astray. They started to curse and blame each other. But what is the use? It is their fault they consoled themselves.

However, a flash of idea twinkled in the mind of Lakshmi and stand up and went to bed room and collected the chip of the film of the camera and wanted scrutinize at Forensic Laboratory at Rajahmundry. She advisedthem "to stay here itself since she herself alone would lead the mission and get the work done". She further advised them "not to reveal or consult with anybody including mummy.

As usual "you both go to the school and if any asked about me you tell that I have gone to attend the music class."She engaged an independent Auto for whole day service. Normally most of the Autos are used as "Share Auto" in the village so that there can be more revenue for the Auto Driver.

She directly went to Forensic Lab spirally meant for Camera snaps by both scanning and exposing with external light to bring out image brighter than earlier. She contacted Dr. Fernandez who is an expert Forensic Lab Technology. He after number of experiments that he knew to bring the image to brighter than the earlier. She had also requested him to remove his mask through auto-graphic technology so that original face can be traced out. Fortunately, the brighter image after erasing the mask from the face of the culprit could be seen. Then on seeing the original face, she got shocked and felt unconscious. With efforts taken by the Doctor Fernandez she woke up and wanted cry. But before other person that too Doctor she controlled herself by sitting aloof for a while and she became attentive to get prepared for the next course action. She went to Mr. Venkat and met him and explained everything including their plan of action etc.

He also got shocked to learn about strange news and wondered for the catastrophe fell on them from within their premises. He is unable to digest calamity they faced. He raised up and wanted to go to police station and give complaint. But she prevented him since if this news becomes viral the fate of their younger sisters will be sealed and instigate them to commit suicide. She took permission with Venkat after sipping tea in the restaurant and went back to home.

On reaching home she combed the entire house to trace the medicine or herbal powdersthat caused them to go in the state of coma. She went to the bed room of her parents and searched his father's pockets and draws of almirah one after another. After a thorough search she could discover innumerable sachets of packets, which started emitting benzoin resin drowsy smoke. She took few pockets and she went to Rajahmundry and gave it for lab analysis.

Dr. said it is "nothing but cocaine with additional mixture of narcotic plant which stimulates the person who consume it into total drowsy sleep and he cannot wake up even after shaking the body at least for 8 to 9 hours and completely come down to senses for an about 10 to 12. It is also obvious for some time he goes into coma when he is in his sixties or when is a diabetic." Doctor said further that "first where from you find these dangerous drugs, as it is most serious offence as per Indian Penal code"

Lakshmi while reacting to the doctor's question said "No sir, I found it in the road while travelling, Please sir sorry I took it out ignorance"

Then Doctor said no matter "you immediately go to drainage canal and throw the remaining pockets there at, otherwise it would be problematic that may lead to so many complications."

Again she called other two sisters for the meeting in her room.

She disclosed all the factors of their rape. On hearing this" bothof the sisters became thunderstruck and started crying". For that Lakshmi requested them to keep silent. She said "at this juncture what would be our next course of action that we should think of at present as this is a peculiar and frightening issue for us as our own father proved an Offender. This is most strange. I have never heard such case. I do not know how to face the society. We are unable to lodge this case with Police or fight in court of law. Our position became so perplexed that neither we inform the matter to our parents or nor keep silent."

Then Saraswathi Jr. said let us go and start consulting with our mother as she is the only person that she can show a way out for this frightened situation. Is it not?"

"Yes" they all said "let us go and consult mother to solve our problem"

At that moment Saraswathi Senior, their mother, came to them and said" what is that you are referring my name for consultation. What is the matter? Please tell me."

Then they narrated the entire terror story and shown the images and the powder that collected from his draw. On hearing this she instantly fell into unconsciousness.

Of course on sprinkling some water she got up and said that "Since the marriage of your brother SeethaRam, your father used to go hither and thither. I noticed his restlessness, but I never imagined that he was after you my Childs! I do not have words to abuse him. He is more than a monster. He is worse than a savage.

"While abusing him she shredded tears after tears, which shows her inability in deciding the fain-hearted solution. And finally she said "You my Childs I am unable to do anything since the issue is so perplexed and complicated. At both ends I am fixed and I do not know who to blame and whom to push out but of course your father is the main person who should be punished at any cost. But how, police, court or any other legal methods cannot be operated here, since the matter of clash is among family members and the result would be your future which will be at stake."

She again said "Let us take time in finding the solution hence you maintain silence for the time being since the smallest action of revenge is taken it would jeopardize the entire issue and our family will be on roads by being abused by the society and for that nobody is prepared to face either you and me or your father and finally we may have to go for honor suicide. That would be final step need to take up, hence kindly give me time."

From the next day onwards the life became normal and all the trio started attending the school without any further complications, except during night times. They used to hear noises of quarrel and abuses from the bedroom of their parents. But having learnt about this they did not ask their parents about the shouting.

For about a lapse of a month all the three Tridevis' noticed that some sort of uneasiness, reeling and vomiting sensations. They again consulted her mother about the uncomfortable feelings. On hearing this news Saraswathi smelt that this would be a case of insemination and she immediately asked them "let us go to the Lady Doctor at Rajahmundry and let us know whether it is a case of pregnancy or digestive problem."

They took a taxi and rushed to the city and landed in the newly opened clinic and consulted with Gynecologist by name Hemalatha who is newly practicing here as physician. She took them the theatre and examined the case. The Doctor brought them to her mother and started congratulating that "Your all three daughters are pregnant hence I congratulate you for having impregnated simultaneously and carrying the same period of one month."

On hearing this second shocking news, she failed to talk but started weeping. The Trios, came to her and consoled her mother not to fear we will tackle the issue ourself. Don't take it serious. Let us first and discuss the matter in the house. They paid the fees and took U turn to their village and entered the house all of four collapsed down in their respective beds. They complain God "Oh. God what a crime we have had done in our past life? Why you are taking revenge against us? Kindly grant us released from this mundane world and take with you? Or tell us what action we take that that monster? Likewise all of them fell on their respective beds and slept while releasing continuous flow tears through their eyelids.But God's face remains as rocky as it was, no movement no blessing or cursing.

Senior Saraswathi became crumbled she has not decided except to get switch off her life. But before taking a strong decision, she called all the three of her daughters. On their arrival she pleaded "to go away from here as father's crime is growing day after day Hence I request you please go away somewhere in the world. Before leaving she also said" My dear Children, you take this letter and give to you Maternal Uncle and if possible stay with them at Kakinada. It would be safe for you both. Take this cover also wherein in I have had written everything about the evils of your father. Though I could have taken decision against your father, by killing him, but I could not do so, since you are hear like my favorite dolls. Now the water is flowing above our heads. I am sorry…..again said I am sorry my princes"….

and she closed her eyes and physically becamesilent. They thought that her mother has gone to sleep, hence they also left the room and reached to their respective rooms. Lakshmi took the kept it in her valet. Letter, desirous of reading it .

Around 5 pm Lakshmi woke up and went to Kitchen, prepared coffee and brought it to her sisters and mother.

First she went her mother's room and asked her to get up from the bed as the time is around six. But no response from her mother. She attempted her throughmaneuvering her, but even then no response. She shouted "O Saraswathi, Oh Durga please come over here on the bed room. But there was no response. She moved to their rooms and shook them to get up and come to see your mother, it seem she has left both us andreachedheavenly abode.

Come fast and see our fate. She prayed the "Oh God what is this punishment. Why are you angry with us? Why you are playing with our innocent lives. Why do not you take revenge with … our bloody father who is the cause for our misfortune, don't you know? If you don't know then why you are called God the protector the preserver etc.? Dog is better than you just because if we throw some chips of food he serves and protect us for the life time? You are none other than a simply a stone who learned to receive only our offerings but doesn't gratitude to help?" She said to other sisters "Let us also take the poison and leave the world to its fate Come on Saru and Durga lets us consume this pesticide and die"

They both said to Lakshmi "be calm let us see and think for the next course of action"

On hearing the sounds from inside the house Ramanujam came in and saw the corpse of his wife lying on the ground. He suddenly called for some nearly villagers and take her to funeral yard and arrange for pyre without waiting. Neither their daughters came and talk to him nor did he go to his daughters to console them. He behaved like rouge with stone heart.

Normally Hindus believe a saying that "Thigh relation will last for ninety years" Here a man who had number of years of thigh with his wife, he is still passive and reluctant to have affection on her service she rendered all the way.

Some laborers attended and took the corpse in the car and dropped the corps on the bed of wooden pieces. Ramanujam came with torch and lit the fire over her body. He stayed there for about half an hour till the head blasted out and moved away.

He went to Godavari and took three dips and changed his dress and came back to clinic and get involved in preparing medicine. It appears strange since he looked calm and silent without any display of emotions on his face. More so heis feeling happy, as noticed from his movements of his face. How strange God only knows (GOK). Another most important item of the event is the son of the diseased has to attend the funeral ritual by sprinkling water by putting hole on the side of the pot. But that son Seetha Ram was neither informed of nor invited to attend the funeral and waited till his arrival before the ritual of Pyre. So strange.

There in the house all the three sisters had pristine bath became fresh started cooked some ritual food (Rolled rice) that is given to the cocks near corps. Ramanujam was informed about the food through his Assistant, then came and took the food and thrown near the funeral area and came back. He did not wait until the cocks came and eat the food. The Hindus particularly Brahmins believe that if the Rice rollers placed near or around the funeral area is totally eaten away by the cocks, thenit would be considered as the dead body is relieved of his/her soul and soul meets to its SuperSoul (Paramatma).

Thus the day went through a strange note that "The sun has disappeared from the sky early making the evening dark. Perhaps he would have puzzled with the strange tradition that the present generation has deviated with age old practice of rituals.

On completing their dinner at night they informed Narayana Swamy about the night dinner is ready for eating. On hearing his Assistants' message, Ramanujam closed the clinic and went to the kitchen and had the dinner and moved to his room for sleeping.

Here in the bed rooms all three sisters slept in the same bed room of Lakshmi. Now they started fearing to sleep in seclusion.

Ramanujam, The Father, thought to engage either one of his daughter for his pleasure, but all the three daughters are sleeping in single bed of Lakshmi. Today being the ritual day, they might have slept in single room and hence he decided to see next day. Even after the bad event has taken place in his house instead showing mourning condolences, this fellow is running after to seek pleasure to satisfy his sex appetite. What a strange person Mr. Ramanujam is?

But Lakshmi, though, sleeping mode, she is observing the movements of her father who came to her bed room for number of times. She is closely watching every movement since she and her sisters laid on her bed. She know that he may attempt a random rape in this night. She could grasp his psychology when he reluctantly took her mother for funeral and hurriedly put on pyre as a formality.

This shows that he doesn't have love or affection on any women even on his wife who was a mate and closely associated with him for the longer than 35 years. This made Lakshmi to develop on her father andcame to a conclusion that here after they sleep in the single bed as a group, so that heredeemed the idea of rape toany of hisdaughter he want. She did not go into sleep as immediately as her innocent sisters went. She tried to call on to her brother Seetha Ram "to go over here and witness how pitiable life they are all   leading here in the village under the guardianship of our father and as our mother also is no more here to safeguard usin the world. We became refugees in our own house! `

We don't know what a peril will fall on us in the shape of Rape on your sisters by your beloved father!"

While murmuring in herself she went into deep sleep. However they could spend their life without being attacked with Rape by their natural guardian. The crescent on sky must have felt relaxed as he could not see the most frightening scene during the last night.

Lakshmi raised as usual in the morning and went to kitchen and cooked breakfast and lunch simul-taneously as she wanted to go meet Mr. Venkat and take his advice in this gruesome situation. She raised all other sisters and served them with Upma and "advised them to go to school as usual and remain there itself and then in lunch time I shall come to you at the interval period and arrange tiffing etc." Don't be panic, I will set right everything hence no worry" Both of the sisters enquired about their elder sisters' welfare and asked to come early before lunch period.

Lakshmi landed in Rajahmundry and went to the College of commerce there at and enquired about Venkateswara Rao, she came to know that he gone to Delhi for lecture to MBA students as an external professor and he is expected to come back by next week. On hearing this news she returned back to her village with heavy heart. She buzzed her mobile Phone to connect Seetha Ram but fail to call on as the response was termed as "Switched off". She came to conclusion that he would havebecome house-son-in-law (Intialludu) instead of normal son in law. Out of one year he came here only once that too in the early months of his marriage. Why? What would be the cause? She firmly said let herself "let me find out. I doubt whether he is in Eluru or got transferred to other place"

Any way she wanted take lead, in the affairs of family, and tackle its pros and cons. She is more worried for the stay here in nights. She started searching through her mind's windows which way is better. Her thoughts or wavering and roaming on all the angles of critical event like "Where to go?" "She thought of even taking the help of Police? But how? The family secrets will immediately be spread like a viral immediately, besides the tendency of their looks with sex appetite more than their father? It would be cruel than their house? And this would more dangerous too as all the family secrets would be bulletined in the entire society?

She felt it is absurd for the time being hence deleted that idea from her mind.

See the fate of these innocent teenaged girls, who are seriously thinking of a shelter in their own village near their own house? Their position is like a "tides are thirsty in its own sea". Then where to go, where to hide? It is not one day or two days, many months or years since the future is mysteryand one know how long it will take to get thefire cooled down? They are shelter less within their own shelter! What a Paradox? What an oddity?

She again started notifying that"Oh God please save us? We are like refugees in our own land? Does' it not look strange to you O God? It is not only myself I am responsible for my sisters too. They are innocent? What a perplexity what ambiguity? The very guardian himself became a Monster in this concrete jungle? Mr. Venkat is also not here then where to go; where to reside? She thought of Seetha-Ram's in-laws at Rajahmundry? But Oh! No. It would be more turbulent?"

We cannot give answers for their investigative interrogation and my brother's position would be in dilemma? However she could stop of at one unit of thought out of innumerable waves of thought. That idea is Venkat's parents who are so good people that they are more than our parents. For the time being it would be better place of shelter. Finally she decided to stay with them along with her two sisters" Again she started doubting about their residence? It must be full of foul smell of leather since his father is a cobbler so it must be full of old shoes, sandals, mules and leather pieces which emit foul Smell? Oh No.It is a kind of punishment for Brahmins, but by living amongst them with that foulsmell would-stillbe better thanthe violent atmosphere prevalent here in our house? However comparatively leather and Non-veg smell would be lesser if we think of that that violent smell?"

"Then why not Choudhry's house? It would comparatively better but there also we may have face rotten atmosphere, since Choudhury's character is twittered as vulgar as our father. Any way Venkat's house looks better for the time being shelter" she said within herself. She took a suit case and took some dress of all her sisters along with her dresses. She also took tiffin carrier to arrange lunch for them at school. She took money from their chests including his father's one, which worked around some 60 thousand along with gold ornaments, perhaps it would be necessary for the time to come?

Lakshmi took her mobile and dialed Venkat for number of times and finally he replied "Hello Lakshmi" How are you? I could not take your permission before leaving Rajahmundry since because the situation was so emergent and I did not find to call on you. Please tell me further course action you would like to take."

Lakshmi explained the events that happened on yesterday day and informed him that she has decided to move your parents' house to have shelter there for this night till you come back from Delhi, since we are not safe here in our house and the reason you know. More so our mother also has left the world leaving us in seclusion. We feel that that is only place to go and take shelter for short period, if you permit what do you say?"

Venkat said submissively that "why not I shall pass on the message immediately. You do not worry, but you see that nobody should see you all going to our house. Right. But I am hesitating to send you all there and the reason you know well ... We are Non-Veg and my father is cobbler. Of course our house is clean and neat except that smell?   No stop, just one second, you do one thing. You all three engage an Auto immediately proceed to my aunt's house   at Rajahmundry whose husband is an Officer in the Commercial Tax Department as A.C.TO. His house is most suitable for you. If you go to our house, your father will not leave in tracing and catch hold of you because it is a small village if you sneeze entire village will get cold."

"Every   moment of the village would be watching every moments of others and this may lead to facilitate your   Father and it would be big issue that may become a fish market, sorry vegetable market!You take a small carry bag where you can keep one or two pairs of your clothes and proceed to Rajahmundry by an auto as immediately as possible and drop at Padmavath Nagar which is nearer to my college. Our uncles' house though look small from outside, it is a 4BHK independent house they all put together are only twoliving in that house.

They are more cultured and have developed urban etiquettes. His   name   is Kondiah, ACTO, Padmavathi Nagar, and Rajahmundry.   Just wait I shall call him through mobile, till then don't take any hasty step." After 10 minutes, Lakshmi received his phone call   through which he stated that "It would be the safest spot where you can hide temporarily till my arrival on coming Sunday and later we can have a detailed discussion over the issue and vestige what steps we need to take. Don't hesitate in taking any help from me and my people. I shall be with you both not only for time being but for life time, if you accept my proposal. Until then you remain in uncle's house without coming out side. Right. Be courageous I am here to share your anguish for life time. You said once that I am a Hero but without you I would be Zero. Make it granted."

On hearing his encouraging exhortation in this crucial time, she considered "his guidance reasonable and praise worthy. Yes it would be right thing to move outside the village and take asylum as suggested by him." But she forgot to ask him about his aunt's position, she said herself "what reply should I give if his aunt starts questioning for our absconding from house because ladies are more meticulous in raising number of objections for receiving us who are absconding from their house.

Hence she gave a call again to Mr. Venkat to get clarified." Luckily he responded immediately and replied all the questions she posedand said "Do not worry dear Lakshmi. I have explained some story inbrief on account of this she may not pose like Kali Matha, everything would go smoothly don't fear and if you have any doubt. You please rush up first and desert from the village. I would be always in touch with you and with my aunt to educate your moments

I am much worried than you all since you are all teenagers and tender to tackle this predicament, any way bye. Be careful while deserting your village since many known persons would come across and dump innumerable doubts and question. Okay"

On hearing his lecture she felt brave and started moving from the house by collecting three plastic carry bags and dumping their dresses. They went out from the back side of the main door and engaged an Auto and pioneered to Rajahmundry directly landed at Kondiah's house as directed by Mr. Venkat. Near main door Venkat's Aunty seen waiting for them. The moment they landed she invited them inside the house and paid the Auto's bill and closed the door. It appeared that they have travelled all the way through not Sun and nowentered in the bright Moon where they expected a motherly affection.

The detective to whom Mr. Ramanujam has appointed could not expect that they would spunk so easily and hence he did not convey any message to his hirer (Ramanujam). He also did not expect that they can disappear from the village like a Tri-Engine Rocket. Of course he was against for this work, but now he felt relieved in chasing them round about 24 hours without proper payment. It was why because that Fellow Ramanujam treated him by dispensing him with right medicine for the disease called HIV. For that gratitude only, he said loudly that"

I served him for so long and strenuous time without any remuneration" I should give thanks to his daughters who were so gentle in their movements but this fellow suspected them unnecessarily and for that reason he appointed him for detecting. Bye Mr. Rogue". Perhaps he may not be knowing actual cause of suspicion. If he actually know about the fact he should have killed him with AK 47 shots.

Here at Rajahmundry, all Trios are being treated with much backing. They breathed easy and feel comfort. Lakshmi said to their sisters "Thank Lord Venkateswara, for having blessed us from getting liberated from the house of Dragon" Both of her sisters responded and felt a sigh of relief. Though all the three are minors god gave an intelligent mind to them to adventure of escaping from the Tyranny without plucking out the prestige of their family both in the village and circle of relative and friends.

All of a sudden Venkat's aunt by name Uoormi-la came and served them with hot Cashew Nut Upma duly sprayed with Pure Ghee. All the trios with great gratitude and tears in their eyes, received it finished within seconds as they were full of hunger and appetite. After finishing the evening breakfast they prostrated down to touch her feet with great indebtedness.

But she shouted and said "No. My dear kids. No it is not good for you to touch others feet. I have discharged my duty. What is there to validate me for the simple act of serving dishes? No you are Stars, you like my daughters or say really daughters from this day on wards for having trusted my brother Venkat and me belonging to Cobbler community who are treated as low grade and Scheduled caste children's"

Then Lakshmi said "OhGod, You said just now that we are your daughters and there is nothing wrong in touching your feet, as you are really entitled for that word "Mother Goddess" Don't say that we upper caste people and you low castepeople. It is only the profession and not preposition that titles that one is washerman, cobbler, barber, Roddy's, Kamma, and Kapus like that. I know your Venkat is not an ordinary man he is a Lord Venkateswara for us. We humans are all One as stipulated by the preamble of UN Constitution. Even in India the same word is being designated in our Indian constitution that All Indians are One, a nd have equal rights, thought they have different duties.

We are Unity in Diversity, my dear Aunt. Likewise we were made as Brahmins since our ancestors had the knowledge of Brahma and we determined as Brahmins. Birth in particular community is not the criteria but it is the creed that makes difference, as stipulated by Vivekananda and

BR Ambedkar.It is all manmade dissection and not godly one. It is all the work of smear interest people who made the untoward casteism. Hence I request Mother not to degrade yourself for God's sake."

Then Uoormila said "Ö My God what brilliant ideas you have all trios. I feel downgraded myself before your opinion. I am sorry I couldn't estimate you properly. That is why our Venkat is showing much reverence and regard to you both. You all are equally gentle both physically and psychologically. You have most modern thoughts. I am really proud of you why because our Venkat is after you. Let God bless you both to get married. I am much impressed for your brief lecture on Casteism which no Philosopher have so far failed to explain in India except Buddha and Carvaka. It is great. Just wait I will come with tea."

No mother said Lakshmi We "are here to serve and we will go in the kitchen and prepare Tea and serve since we feel privileged for your love and affection you are demonstrating over us. We will be serving for life time if you order. Yes Mother really."

Uoormila said "Then wait I shall go first in the kitchen and see that you are served with variety of tea, in which your mother's sugar and my tea powder so that you sip the taste of your mother's affection with honey bite. That's it? It is an order for my being your foster mother. Moreover this is the time your uncle comes from office."

Suddenly, the sound of calling Bell roared spontaneously confirming her words that Uncle Kondiah has just arrived. He wished all of them to feel comfortable in the house, since Venkat's words are Order for us"

Then all the three went and touched his feet for blessing. He was accomplished with shock for their behavior and said "God bless you my children, god bless you. This is an unexpected regard you gave me. I am really feel proud of you all. You look really like Earthly Angels. What Venkat explained of you, you proved more than his words. Really surprising. Please take this gift and enjoy." He gave one sweet Box for each one of them.

They, conveyed their thanks for his affection-ate reward. They went inside and" brought Tea by the time he returned from bath for getting refreshed. While seeing the Tea in their hands he said where your Aunt is?"

He did not see Uoormila who is behind Lakshmi, hiding as she want to know his reaction? Then she came with tears in her eyes and said Ï am here, Don't you. Have not felt my presence? Seeingtheir delightful and entertaining conversation,

Lakshmi and her sister felt introverted and left the scene. But Uoormila, however, called them back and said, "See your uncle is so childish that he doesn't know etiquette. He is your father like and don't feel like timid. You are at liberty call him as your own father as you had attributed me a designation of Mother. See my dear husband garu, I have approved them as my daughters. Any objection?"

" Good. But not only good very good or gooddest? Why now? When I entered in the house I have seen them and their innocent looks, then itself I have decided to adopt them as my daughters? Don't you believe? Yes my dear we do not have any children for that matter and they are the right persons to be designated as "our daughters" by law. Am I right?"

She said you are hundred and ten percent right. I appreciate and congratulate you for having selected them as our daughter."

All of a sudden a phone call triggered and going on whistling. Kondiah lifted the phone and said "Hello. Who is it?" From the other end Venkat's voice said It ismy uncle, Venkat. Have you received those girls from Dhavaleshwaram, victims of unusualstrange fate?"

"They have come here and are feeling happy. Just talk to your Aunt"

On receiving his phone "she said, Hallow Venkat Your "Three Sisters "have come. And they are all happy and one more thing is that we have been elevated as Father and Mother ever since their arrival. They are so nice and innocent. You come first and then I shall explain in detail. Okay".

Here in his Empire, Ramanujam is seems to have been singledout. Nobody is there to serve him either Coffee or food. He questioned himself "where this dirty kids have gone. Entire house is looking as barren and bats are going to shift their house to have their better residence here "Okay let them go I do not care. Let me see how long they stay out, one day or other they come over by begging food and shelter" He called his assistant Narayana to prepare tea and food for the night". His assistant said sorry Mastaru. I don't know cooking. If you want I shall get the meals parcel, if you give 100 rupees?

Ramanujam gave the money to get one meal parcel from the Brahmins hotel and could say himself "that one day is over to spend."

Next day morning, Seetha Ram and his wife Radhika paid visit to Ramanujam to enquire about the welfare of his family members. He knocked the door and door got automatically opened. Both entered the house and saw none. It has become like devils' work shop. It was mainly due to not paying attention for cleaning since long period. It doesn't look a Brahmin's house but house of cobblers. Spider's nests are fully spread on around the house. It is so dirty that he could think to stay there. Radhika, took the sweeper stick and cleaned the entire house. She cleaned all the corners of walls and sprinkled water toremove the thickened dust on the walls. She entered the kitchen and took milk and prepared hot tea and served to her husband.

Seetha Ram is getting wild hour after hour and shouted against his three sisters and said in himself" Dirty rogues, how and why they failed to keep their house uncleansed. What about mother, she is also not seen here since weeks I think. His anger touched the maximum degree of temperature. BP also raised on seeing the dusty condition of his house.Mother is also not seen here. Where else she can go? What happened to this house? The house appears to be the residence of devils. He shouted and went to his father's clinic.

He found that his father is seriously preparing the medicine. He wanted to interrogate him, but decided to not to disturb him now at this juncture, since most of the patients are in queue for consulting and taking medicine.

The moment he entered the house his house, Radhika handed over a list of vegetables and other provisions like Rice, Dal, oil Wheat Atta. Seetha Ram went to market and marketed the provisions immediately and handed over to his wife to prepare food as he is feeling hungry. She went to the kitchen and prepared tasty dishes out of the Vegetables he bought. She prepared Sambar, Rasam, Curd, Papad and Ghee.   It was about 8 pm, and hence he went to the clinic to bring his father for supper meal. The moment he saw Seetha Ram, his father Ramanujam felt ease and asked "When and how did you enter the house? Has my daughter in law arrived along with you?"

Seetha Ram said politely that"she has also come and prepared fine dishes for you. One thing Dad, where is Mummy and where does our sisters trios went?" Thus he raised innumerable questions and for that Ramanujam simply said "Let us complete our Supper first. Then I will let you know the facts and figures either to day night or tomorrow morning as I am dam tiered so wait until then?

"Right!" Said Ram. Hecouldn't speak further and he simply moved to the kitchen and order to serve the meals.

Ramanujam wished her and said "What Thalli (mother), are you keeping well.   I thought you have my grandson by now. But you look barren so far. Why what is the matter? If not why? Please tell me I have good medicine for you since I am a specialist in Gynecological problems. It is my left hand business for me to cure such ailments"

Seetha Ram said yes Dad whenever she get menses she used to discharge more than normal. Hence all the way I came to you both to see you and consult with you about this issue."

Ramanujam said "Don't worry it will setright. Don't be perturbed, my Chitty Thalli It should be set such problems at an early stage itself or else other problems will arise. From now itself I shall give medicine don't worry".

Radhika Said "Yes dad, I shall follow your guidance. Come on first take food"

Ramanujam said 'just wait I shall bring medicine kit now itself and start taking the course from today onwards and if you go on taking it for about two weeks, everything would be set right. Give your hand first I will diagnose the problem, if any, by reading your purse rate"

She gave her right hand to him. He took her hand started reading her pulse rate for one minute. Then said "nothing to worry, It will be set within a month. Another thing is, you tell me the regular date of menses so that I can prepare a calendar of medicine for consumption.

She said "It is 10th every month, uncle"

Then he started calculating some drawingson the paper and said finally "I am sure to say that you would be conceived within your course of next menses. Take it as granted

Ramanujam went to his clinic and brought a set of small powder pockets folded with. He said now itself you take the medicine now itself before food and then another pocket while going to bed. Keep avoid sleeping with your husband at least for one week. After completing your course you observe during menses and if you notice that it is normal then you stop using the medicine. Otherwise if you notice any abnormality you repeat the course of using the medicine until further date of menses, and I think by that time everything must set right. To be on safe side I have given three months course.

He said "the first pocket which is separately packed in pink color paper you use it at bed time to day itself. This would be first and last dose. I am giving another medicine to suit male one so as to match the treatment. Next day onwards you use it regularly at bed time. One more thing after using the first dose, you better sleep in separate room and not beside your husband and this is an important instruction that you should obey squarely, since during consumption of this first dose you should not get matedwith your husband and that is why I am advising you to sleep inseparate room. Like that you continue for two menses periods"

Ramanujam after finishing is supper, went tohis bed room and started reading a newspaper and finally he slipped into sleep on bed.

Here Radhika and Seetha Ram also took meals and strolled in Verandah for some time and seceded into sleep in separate bed room as suggested by his father. Radhika took the Pink packed powder dose before her going to bed time. Just after ten minutes she noticed the drowsiness and slipped into deep sleep. Suddenly after 2 hours, Ramanujam entered her bed room and started the same old practice of Porn with his daughter in law also.

He opened her boobs and started sucking and slowly put his cock in her pussy and raised to pitch of fucking, removed it and put it around her face, lips, around boobs. He made turned and inserted his cock on back of buttocks and rubbing her entire body with his erected cock for nearly half an hour and finally put back in her pussy and gave heavy to heavy shots and finally ejected his honey in to her honey pot. He got up from the bed and set her as is where is and moved away to his bed room silently and went to sleep.

Next day Radhika could wake up after heavily shaking her body by Seetha Ram. She felt still drowsy and slowly went bath roomand became fresh. She told to her husband that " I do not know what happened it was dream like situation where in you came to me and started to do that act, but I could not resist and rose up, but enjoyed whole activity as a person mesmerized."

Seetha Ram said "I too felt drowsy and slept for whole night without getting in senses as against my regular habit to wake up once in the night time to go to bath room to attend the natural calls." He further said, the powder that my dad gave worked so effectively that I never had such a deep sleep without being disturbed in midnight."

" See Our Dad's medicine is so powerful that it would certainly work for the treatment ofany kind of decease."

But Radhika is in different world and going on thinking about the happening in the last night. She felt in her dreams that she faced the powerful attacksexually, whichshe never experienced with Seetha Ram ever since the marriage.She is so happy after using that powder. She experienced the feeling as if she is roaming in the Heavenly abode.

On completing breakfast both went back to Visakhapatnam. He could not enquire abou t his mother and Sisters, but presumed that they would have gone to our Aunt's house at Rajahmundry. Hence he could not inquire about them and simply passed on.

On the very next day they took permission and boarded an Auto to Rajahmundry. But on the way he failed to enquire about his mother and his sisters. However consoled that I can collect information later from his father himself.

Next day Ramanujam felt the necessity of a cook and servant boy so assist both in clinic and in his house. However he contacted his Assistant and asked whether he knows cocking? He smartly said "No. Mastaru, I do not know cooking. If you so desire I shall get Meals parceled from nearby Hotel as the owner of the Mess is Brahmin."

" I know, take this money and bring two meals parcel, and asked him to give more mango chutney and one extra Papad."

As it was two thousand Rupees Note, that fellow got wonderful idea of skipping away to Rajahmundry and settle there to look after a suitable job as Server in the Posh Hotel Anand Regency as it was a dream hotel to work in the Regency Hotel He said himself "This Ramanujam fellow is a rogue. He is always after lady patients and check with Stethoscope as if he is a MBBS doctor, at the sensitive parts of the women.

He said himself that "He used to take more work from us and pay lessor salary. Most miser fellow on the face of the earth, I think. I wanted leave this fellow as early as possible. Luckily I could take 2000 Note for the first time in the life, so let me skip this fellow and settle there in the City. All the while he is used to provide "grass" for me to eat". Thus he left to the city by a share auto of Rs.5/ per head.

Ramanujam waited for about an hour, but that fellow did not turned up so far. He, felt that he must have fled to Rajahmundry after seeing the 2000 note. Okay, he decided himself to go to that mess opened recently. He took meal with double quota of Mango Pachhadi and curd. One of his known person wished him and said "Namaste" Panthulu garu and said" What is this your taming your meal here in the mess. Are your family members out of station and gone pilgrimage?"

Ramanujam said "No Not that all of them have gone tomy son's house at Eluru, but I could not go there just because of the heavy of inflow of patients from outside our state. That is it?" He moved on to his house and another known person came across to him "How is that you are in this mess? Of course Auntie is no more but you have three girls' children? Are they not attending you to look after you for food?"

Ramanujam gave the same reply and moved on to his house. Suddenly he recollected one thing and said to him" You Srinivasan, I know that you have one cooking maid who is a Brahmin, near your area. Is she stillavailable?"

For that he responded obediently "why not? She is available and she is at present working in our friend's house ….I think his name is Raghavachari. Do you require on temporary basis or for a long period." Ramanujam said "I know Raghav who is also a Vaishnavite, please ask him to spare her I shall paymore salary than others. Right. Kindly pass on the information to her also."

Srinivasan while cycling his bike promised that he would arrange her.

He started thinking" that Brahmin maid who is expert in cooking Vegetarian dishes, if accepts, to work for me it would be most delightful for me as she becomes a seneseshu Rambha and Bhojeshu Matha. Yes right. I shall keep her in my house as a permanent maid instead of going to marry another lady which will costs social boycott and forego heavy exchequer in the name of the share of property after his death. I need not invite my son or daughters for the marriage. This would be very admirable step for me" Likewise he went to the house and took some steroid power and went to sleep"

On the other end Mr. SeethaRam is busy with his family's developments and welfare. He was blessed with a female child and now she is crawling and stepping her budding steps and on seeing her he forgot his entire past and now is busy with his daughter and his lovely wife. Though he received so many calls from his sisters and his father he used to switch off the phone so that other party would feel that he must be busy with his office work. But of course he sincerely attends both in laws calls and replies or discuss in detail with great pleasure enthusiasm. He proved the aged saying that" Wife is Bellam and Mother is Allam (Wife is sweet and mother is savory).

SCENE 5

SOCIAL SUPPORT TO THE VICTIMS

Mr. Venkat came from Delhi as per schedule and he went to Aunt's house so as to see the fate of his beloved Trios. He felt so anxious that he became restless to see Lakshmi's face first then he can take relaxed breathe. Fortunately Lakshmi opened the door with the same anxiety and concern for Venkat. They wanted to hug each other but manners did not permit them.

She shouted that see my mother "Venkat has come all the way from Delhi. Come on." Both his aunt and uncle could study her pulse and said "Oh. Yes Welcome Mr. Venkat all of us are waiting here sincelast midnight. Said his uncle on seeing her face. Lakshmi felt that she is over acting, but finally she could control herself and she coolly went to Kitchen and brought Tea for him. Venkat is so happy to witness "happy atmosphere in the house." He in his heart conveyed his thanks and regards to his Uncle and Aunt for accommodating the three Sisters in their house. However he could not control emotions and said, "Sorry aunty I troubled you in taking care of the Trios."

Then Uoormila said "Why sorry? All of them are my daughters (in-law) you know. Your Uncle also paid his compliments for my decision, you know."

Venkat smiled from his heart and appreciated them for their grace and mercy and openly shouted "Oh My god one more god and goddess are living in this house kindly accord them much boons. He went to his Aunt prostrated and touched her feet and then to his uncle. He said "Oh my Aunt I don't have words to praise you both for your blessings shown to these poor victims"

Then his Aunt and Uncle responded by saying "why Victims" What is the matter please inform us in detail. Their looks seen more exclamatory".

Venkat narrated entire story to them bit by bit. How their father used to give-deep-sleeping dose, before attempting rape, and how violent molestation he used to conduct with his own daughters, which recalls the name of Bonobo in such atrocities. It is also informed that "he used to give sleeping dose to his wife so that she never wakes up until morning. He even raped his last daughter who is studying only 6th class.For that matter all the three are minors below 18 years.

His behavior of rape is comparatively referred to pedophile like Bonobo. The powder he used was not other than Mixture of Cocaine and Heroin.

I was personally there in the Forensic Lab and scan. Such atrocities he used to implement over his own innocent and immature daughters! More so he is a staunch orthodox Brahmin. Then tell me how anybody can tolerate such things. Their mother on learning that all the three are pregnant on same date and same time, she got shock and took some poisonous pesticides and passed away. This made the Tri-Devis to escape from that house and appealed me to provide shelter or else we will also join with our mother by committing suicide.

Their only brother is busy with his new family at Eluru and he failed to respond for umpteen numbers calls they dialed. In these circumstance what should be the response one can expect from those cultured and intelligent children of uncultured savage father since every night became a frightened and panic stricken life they were forced to spend. Hence I suggested them your name and house them so that they can take shelter as refugees at least by using my name. So please tell me have I done any wrong thing in recommending your house for shelter?"

On hearing his narration, both his Uncle and Aunt became spell-bound and shocked. His uncle Sri Kondiah said "I wonder that such fathers are there living in this world, Particularly in India that too from most revered community of Brahmans. What is that their Vedic God is doing? How could he create such a nasty father? I have never heard or seen rogues. Mr. Venkat, my brave brother son you did a right thing in recommending our house. You will have full support from our side. Don't worry let us think and have an active plan of action to take on those innocent children? See their fate, they look beautiful in all angles, born in a highly regarded community, to most rich and prosperous father. But they are living in deplorable and afflicted condition they are forced to live?" Both his uncle and Venkat observed the condition of Uoormila, she looks fainted without any voice or notice. Then Venkat sprinkled a bit of water on her face and then she could come to her senses.

She demonstrated her high pitchof woe sum emotions and started weeping. She said "I do not have words to explain those poor girls situation. It is most heartbreaking condition that no one should face in the world. If I were there in that situation I would have used kitchen knife and cut his throat and would have seen his end. Most astonishing and rare situation prevailed over these innocent Children. This shows that there is no such thing God to be worshipped. He is only a Rock structured human figure and nothing else!"

"I have considered them as my own children and hence I have decided to give them a fair and comfortable life, as it is my duty to do so now at this time what do you say my dear Pati Dev?" Said Uoormila.

Soon after the discussion, Uoormila went to the bedrooms of the Trios. For her dismay she found none. She searched both kitchen, toilet and other bed rooms. But none was noticed. She shouted "Venkat" come here the Children are seems to have departed from the house, go outside and take a bike and go on searching either at bus stand or edge of the Godavari bridge. Both Venkat and Kondiah went through their bike started searching inch by inch of the surrounding area of house.But nowhere are they noticed. They raided to Bus stand, Railway station even nearby Temple. But they were seen passing through Godavari Road-Cum Rail Bridge, with the carry bags filled with clothes. Venkat shouted "Lakshmi wait we are coming. Don't take any drastic decision. Stop please".

They were about to Jump in torrent Godavari. Kondiah raided the vehicle with bulletspeed and could catch hold of them and picked up from the parapet walls of the bridge. They said loudly" What is this? You are running out from us and the very life itself. Are you mad? We are discussing about you since the morning about the course of action to take up and protect you all. But you fools you have betrayed us and escaped to commit suicide? This is too much.

I never expect from you this type of hasty decision to commit suicide" But he saw spate of tears falling like from their eyes. Sorry I can understand you. I know that you are self-respecting personalities but there must be reason also. Here we are all jointly thinking about a better way out from this critical situation, do you know?"

They all broke out with tears and said" Sorry Venkat we have caused much trouble to you all. We felt that on hearing our spoiled condition what would Uncle and Aunt think of us, they may form a bad opinion about us and hence we thought of embracing mother Godavari. You people are so good that we doubted you that you may reject us as a scrap, since in our community the spoiled one are never received us with honor though they are their own offshoots. Hence we thought of abandoning you and join with Mother Godavari. In our community for simple menstruation women will be out casted for 7 days and make them as untouchable commodity and…"

Then Venkat said "stop your lecture, come inside. Forget about it all and go to bathroom and get fresh sothat we can have breakfast prepared by your "Mother". All of them laughed and moved away for their respective duties.

After breakfast Aunty served them with a cup of

tea to each and went through to clean the Trios Bedroom. There she found one big letter is lying on the Teapot. She took the paper and presented to Venkat to read. On seeing the letter Venkat said" this is written in English. Okay I will read said Venkat and started reading.

Waiting, debating	Just thinking het is out there
Weeping contemplating	With another girl called sister
On whether or not I	And one Sister after another
Should be saying	It make me want to hurt
He took one thing	They probably must be scared
Which I can never get back	I have no business
It just goes to show	I have no scars
The real humans lack	But taking my and others Virginity
Trust was a thing	Was like taking our hearts
My mom gave to him	Why would he do this
Not knowing the Monster He	What did me and they do?
Hides within	I can take my mind of him
I lay down for sleep with cocaine	I don't know others what to do?

Knowing the moment is coming	*Picture perfect memories*
When he finally breaks through	*Are not images I see*
I am hurt and bleeding	*When I took back and think*
Ignoring my drowsy pleading	*Of me and my younger one*
Does he care?	*I see his face*
Does it bother him?	*Flash in my Mind*
Knew there was more than a thing	*Smiling his ugly smile*
He put inside me	*I wish I was blind*
Other than grim	*He is none other than our father*
Like a Rod penetrating	*We got what a fate?*
Many nights have past	*No shelter even a gate*
And I am still perturbed	*Decided to dip in River in spate*
By the Mess he sprinkled	*O Kalikill him with Trident in hate*
All things in world are disturbed	*By Lakshmi and Sisters*

On learning this essence of the Poem, all of the members shouted with great appeal "once more".

How briefly and gently narrated her agony with due rhythm. "Oh Lakshmi you are great. You are only a tenth class student but how is that you could penned such heart touching poem. It is so nice to know you better continue your writings so that you can put in dark other poets of world. You better make it a career in the cult of literature. Oh I am sorry about your education. I think the examination date is shortly due. Have you got Books?

Lakshmi informed that "I have books with me. If you don't mind kindly arrange any school so that they can enroll me in SSC (CBSE) class on payment. See I have this much money for the time being so you please see that of us are admitted in the respectively classes."

Yes my dear "I shall certainly arrange. But don't give that money I shall sent you out if act like this. You all are our daughters and we are you parents. Keep that money with you only. Don't draw barriers between us with money. Right? "

Uoormila said "No my dear Child, No. We are almost an ordinary humans like you and nothing other than that. It is our privilege that we got tailor made gentle children in our barren life. No further appreciations please"

Then all the three took her feet embraced with

prayer.

On witnessing this emotion filled scene both Kondiah and Venkat felt delighted and ecstatic. Joy filled tears fell down form their eyes too.

Then Laxmi said "I am sorry and feel hailed that we could see God and Goddesses now on earth in this house. What more we want our life is sure to attain salvation and merge into the Paramatma the heavenly abode?"

All of a sudden she called on him and said "we three have the major problem and that one is getting ourself aborted. Let us go to some Gynecologist and drain down this burden. He along with his aunt took them and requested the Doctor to" arrange for abortion at the earliest possible."

Doctor said "Yes, I am ready to abort them, but permission of either their husbands or parents is required. Then Uoormila said I am their mother I am ready to sign wherever you want. Please do it earlier. Then Doctor arranged abortion and cleaned their Uterus with DNC process and said they are Okay. Entire process took about an hour. Doctor advised them rest at least for two days. She also prescribed few tablets for administration. Uoormila paid the fees and took the trios and left the clinic.

Next day Venkat arranged admission in a

Private School on payment of due fees. All the three sisters wrote examination and got passed their examinations including SSC by Lakshmi. She stood to in the School. Likewisethe Intermediate education also completed by Lakshmi, first Year Junior college by Saraswathi and 10th by Durga. Almost three years completed.

SCENE 6

PRESENT OVER AFTER 4 YEARS OF FUTURE

Lakshmi is now studying B. Com final year, Saraswathi 2nd year B.Sc. and Durga in 1st Year B.Sc., with the back up support of Mr. Venkat, Uoormila and Kondiah. No untoward incidents took place in the lives of the three Sisters. They came to learn that his brother Seetha Ram has been posted as Branch Manager SBI Visakhapatnam.

Lakshmi, now and then used to pay respects to both Aunt and Uncle including Venkat for their continuous support both economically and socially. Aunt Uoormila used to pay much attention on three sisters as if they are her own offshoots. There is no need to say about Venkat. Kondiah became a godfather to them. All of them have intermingled as one family members.

The ruthless and uncultured father of the Tridevis seems to have failed to enquire about his three daughters. It is also learned that he has an affair with his servant maid who presently took over the Ramanjam's house under her control and started ruling it is ruling house. Ramanujam is not bothered about his son also. However he used to pay visit to

Mr. Koteeswara Rao father of Radhika, at Rajahmundry. But Koteeswara Rao, now a days did not pay attention to the Ramanujam and his family member except is Son-in-Law Seetha Ram. He is interested only with his daughter's life. Now they have one 5 years daughter and one year old son. Koteeswara Rao used to visit Visakhapatnam now and them to look after his daughters and her child's welfare. Ramanujam is singled out by all the members of his family. Of course he is happy with his unmarried wife who is his servant maid.

Seetha Ram also remained aloof with his family members. He didn't pay any attention towards his sisters. Neither phone call nor personal visits to Dhavaleshwaram. Now Rajahmundry became a center point to all of the family members of Ramanujam.

Lakshmi seems to have attempted Bank Probation Officer's post and fortunately she stood first and posted as Probation Officer in Andhra Bank, Rajahmundry. And other two sisters are now on the verge of completing their Degrees.

Venkat became Asst. Professor in the same college of Commerce. Chiranjeevi son of Koteeswara Rao, now became Soft wear Engineer and working in US, somewhere in Texas. Ajay and Vijay sons of Raamanna Chaudhary seems to have changed their profile and now they are popularly known as Real Estate Owners and they have earned billions. They too are ready for getting married it is so because their father is searching for financially sound party who have single daughter so that the entire property can be clubbed with his property and expecting his status to reach the level of N.T Rama Rao, Film idol, Chief Minister of AP etc.

Likewise the life of all the three families have settled well in their respective jobs and businesses. Venkat's Parents have switched over their nativity to Rajahmundry itself and they have taken the Agency of Bata Shoe Company. Now the problems lies with Lakshmi and her Sisters only.

Venkat seems to have put forth a proposal that he wanted to marry Lakshmi irrespective of her cast and creed and virginity or spoiled but he loved her since the beginning of the occurrence of the horrible events in her house. Though his aunt and uncle accepted the proposal, Lakshmi should think of the proposal in detail as she is matured enough and she is now around 20 years of age, she is major now.

Her   objection is "let the marriage of her two sisters is fixed then we would be free of any encroachment therewith. Her view is our Indian society is not in a position to adopt inter caste religion and hence it would affect the relationship her brother

Seetha Ram and others. She knows it pretty well the trend of the present society which behave like dog and whenever some chips are thrown it keeps quiet and if not, it used to point out the smallest error that we commit. So first let us derive a strong conclusion then only we can go for marriage. We cannot forecast its modus operendi."

"Some time they may say it is most encouraging aspect that they have faced the challenges of society and proved their metal and for some time, if any untoward incident occurred then they start commenting that "see the repercussion of the intercast marriage and its damage that took place in this way." We do not know we people of this cultured and traditional society when they would they forget and invite the progress taken there at. Most of the members of the society will be searching for the errors or untoward incidents, like Divorce or Death or Accident or natural calamities, they would directly attribute to the even that this must be the result of the deviation of the caste system. Let us call all the members of family including their sisters for a sitting and discuss the issue. What would you say Venkat?"

Venkat said "Right. Let the other members of family members know It and give their consent on this issue. It would be the right mechanism for deciding the issue. "Again Venkat said" let us sit on the coming Sunday Right, because uncle would also be here as he has been transferred to Kakinada Office."

Before his leaving, Lakshmi said "one important information I wanted to inform you that our two sisters were very particular to get marry with Ajay and Vijay who have now changed and running a Real Estate business here in Rajahmundry itself. So why cannot we ask their present opinion which would be helpful to solve the issues that gulfed with us. What do you say?"

Venkat said "It is Okay for me but the problem would be with their father, who is fortifying for heavy dowry? You also know his conduct?"

She said "Yes Of course. He was crazy of money. But now I don't think he is of same view. Okay. Why not we meet those Ajay and Vijay in their office and draw their opinion?"

Venkat Said "Right. I have got my own doubt."

Lakshmi said "what doubt?"

Venkat opined that " Doubt means not onthose twins, but my doubt is with Saraswathi and Durga, who may have any infatuation with anybody in their college or otherwise."

"Yes" that would be fine. Let us take their consent too before going those Twins of Shylock" she said.

Venkat moved away riding his bike.

Lakshmi used think of his brother, Seetha Ram. Why he is so aloof and maintaining distance since his marriage. Any way she tried to call on him through phone but phone is ringing and going one ringing.....................finally she could receive sweet words of"Hello who is this?" he said.

She said "Hello Ram, I am Lakshmi, where are you? How are you? How is your health? How is our sister-in-law? Have got any issues? If so who are they, female or male? If female how is she? If male how does he look? If both how are they both? Are they going to School? If going to School in which class they are studying in? Have any time gone to our village? If so when?"

Then Ram replied "Oh my dear sister I am in Vizaq in State Bank of India as a Manager? My health is of course alright? Your sister-in-Law is in house and she is also keeping good health. We have one female Child and she is of 4 years old and studying Lower Kinder Garden. She is most cute and smart like you during your childhood. She became chatter-box, most funny and entertaining. We do not have any male baby yet. Yes I had been to father twice somewhere around fours and later two years back. He is fine. All of you were missing for the both the time of my visit. We were told that you areall in Rajahmundry and executing studies in some boarding school. I also came to know that our mother died of heart failure. And now give me answer for my all questions? What are you and our other sisters doing? I think you must have completed graduation. What about our Saru and Kali? More so where are you studying, is it in Rajahmundry or Kakinada. Dad did not give full details."

In reply she wanted to explain all the turbulent occasions we faced, she did not reveal this things but only said that "We are all fine. I have completed My B.Com and got selected as PO of Andhra Bank. Now at present working in Andhra Bank Branch Rajahmundry itself. Saru and Durga are in second and final year of B.Sc. degree course, here itself. But one thing tell me I made so many nearing about 100 calls during these six years, but you never responded, and every time I gave call the response would be "switched off". Any way by the grace of Almighty, you are traced finally. We felt very bad for your absence. Any way how are your in laws?"

Ram said in his responding call that "What so many calls? It is how and why the reply came as "switched off" No never. Something must have gone wrong, but still I am doubtful. I will contact your Vadina in the evening respond you again. One thing Lakshmi, have you got any proposal of getting married, here my colleague is there, very good boy. Recently joined as PO in our Bank. He is a Brahmin, has good status parentally. I shall contact father if you said Okay for him."

Lakshmi said "No. Ram don't be so hasty. We can have leisure discussion about this. You better avoid our Father for the time being. However I want to let know that I have loved one of my Village colleague who is now working as AssistantProfessor of Commerce. He did CA also. But he is hailing from Scheduled Caste."

"How is that? Is he belongs to S.C.? How can you think like that? Don't you know we are Brahmins?" Reluctantly said Ram.

"HI Brother, cool down please cool down. What do you say we are Brahmins? Then what about you? You also married a non-Brahmin girl? Have forgot? We all know about this? But we maintained silence. And we also know that your Father in law is Sudra (Kapu) and wife is Christian. Perhaps Daddy do not know all this things, but we detected their identity when we went in their Store room. But he kept this in secret till the marriage is over. If you don't know, kindly know it now or ask your better half about this?"

Then Ram said "Oh! Is It? I am also not aware of these facts of cast or statusduring the alliance and marriage. I knew that he managed to camouflage the fact. I could know this only three years ago. OK carryon your alliance. From my side no objection. I would also inform my in-laws to meet you for anything they required. It seems my brother in law who is in States has expressed his willingness to marry our Saru. Hence I am desirous of informing you about my father in law. And one more thing I heard that our father has ties with some servant maid and both are residing in the same house. Now she changed her status from servant maid to Boss of the house and she ruling it like a queen. But I do not know why he has done like that? If you know the reason please inform."

Lakshmi said I don't know all these things we are all out of that Village since 6 years. Hence I do not know anything about our father. Any way we will meet you any time here if you go over here either for Function or any important occasion. Meanwhile I would gather information about Chiranjeevi. I will collect opinion from Saru and I shall pass on the same to her."

Thus this during extensive discussion so many facts and so many events came to the surface that made the lines of relationship cleared.

Lakshmi felt somewhat valiant and bold. All the while she was gloomy and passive. Now she felt happy to learn that someone who is blood related is there in this world other than her villainous father.

In the evening all of the three sisters met and discussed the about their brother and his family. Lakshmi informed everything about his family. She asked Saraswathi "Are you still in favor of marrying the Chiranjeevi brother in law of our brother? You know he had been our house in the village and squarely perceiving you. Now Ram asked me about your secret love among you both. Isn't?" Saraswathi gently smiled and said "If you have no objection, I am ready. I am responsible to you onlybut not bothered from our brother Ram."

Lakshmi said let our brother come here. He said that he would be visiting during Dasahra Holidays then we discuss. Now I have to search for Durga. What Durga have you anybody in your mind?"

Durga said, "of course I have, but I need some more time that I have to complete my Degree and settle in some job and thirdly I have to dis charge one more duty which I will let you know later at the right time.........?

Lakshmi said" What is that duty? Is it a secret? My attitude is how long we depend upon Aunty and Uncle. Let us have our own residence. We should not be further burdened on them."

"Oh you what burden, what dependency etc. you are talking Madam. I warn you now itself that you should not feel yourself as burden on us. I have adopted you "with Manasa Vacha (whole heartedly and with due broadcasting. So don't rise repeat those words hereafter? I became your mother and you my daughters traditionally. That is all? What more you want? Do you require decree to that effect?"

" Sorry Mummy. Once again sorry. It is so because......" Laxmi was telling, but suddenly Uoormila interfered and pressed her mouth and once again "Stop no excuses. That is it?

All of the Trio said jointly with tears shedding that" what Aunty. OK Sorry Thalli? Very much sorry?

"Yes come to the point.Today I have prepared special dish with Cashew Nut Upma with Garelu specially meant for you. I think Venkat also join you as his college duty might have completed by now"

The moment her dialogue is completed the calling bell alarmed with sweet tone.

Uoormila opened the door and Venkat is present as she predicted.

Come on you have incarnated here. She served the Upma and Special Garelu. All of them took chairs in the open terrace and started conducting conference on the issues of the Trios'.

Lakshmi being an earning member inaugurated the conference by saying that I have contacted mybrother Seetha Ram finally to day morning. This is the biggest achievement in my gruesome life for the past 4 years. I tried to contact him nearly century times but failed. So thus the first battle with society that I could won. I had a detailed talk with him through my dial and discussed in detail.

I came to know "that he is blessed with a lovely and cute female baby and she is running 4 years or so and going to School to study LKG. He is in Vizaq working as Branch Manager State Bank of India in Madhuravada. And he promised to visit us during Dasahra Holidays. I learned through discussion that my father has his wife-cum-servant maid.

"When presented my proposal before my brother he invariably objected for my alliance with Venkat on the basis of caste difference between me and Venkat. But I questioned him how about his alliance, you being Brahmin you married the girl of Sudra community, you violated the social contract norms that has been practiced since centuries.

For that he tendered his lorry full sorry's. Then only he put down his head and said I would be meeting you shortly.

In this connection Venkat started saying that" I have one good news. I have contacted Mr. Koteeswara Rao and Sri Ramanna Chaudhary came forward to perform their Son's marriage with Saraswathi and Durga respectively" On hearing this good news all most all of the family members including Uoorvasi and Kondiah. They have also expressed their willingness for not taking Dowry.

Then Venkat said "let us attempt to complete these two targets by next year end since the two sisters will complete their Education"

Mr. Kondiah has also accepted the proposal and expressed his commitment of Marriage celebration of these two foster daughters from his pocket.

Then Lakshmi finally started to spell out a concluding speech of the conference by saying that "I am thankful of Mr. Venkat, Uncle and Aunty, without whom we sisters would not have survived in this world. I would like to pay three millions thanks. They are not only great humans but they proved that they are Dieties to whom one should salute and worship. I never expected our present society is filled with such good philanthropic members also."

SCENE 7

SELF EFFORT ELEVATED TO STARDOM

Slowly two years elapsed and lost their identity by inviting a new year to take up the events that are happening. Lakshmi got posted as Branch Manager AryaPuram, Rajahmundry.

Saraswathi got selection as Sub-Registrar, Registration department at Rajahmundry itself, after writing Group II Examination conducted by APPSC. And Durga is still in plan of searching jobs, since she has completed her B.Sc. Degree just recently. She has written some Service Commission Examinations relating to Group I Grade-A posts. Results and Interview process are still awaited to get completed about her specific Job. So lines are clear for arranging marriage of theses Trios.

Venkat purported much efforts in convincing the parents of Chiranjeevi, Ajay. Koteeswara Rao said "10 lakh Dowry and 30 Tolas Gold in marriage need to be gifted. My son Chiranjeevi is earning around a crore per annum. When compare to the status of her brother he is only a Manager in the Bank drawing about 10 to 15 lakhs per annum. Then compare and say how much I lose in the in the name of Dowry. I was expecting at least 50 lakhs cashand 30 Tolas for my son."

On hearing this Venkat got wild in his heart, but he controlled his emotions and said "See my dear Uncle Saraswathi is also working as Sub-Registrar here in Rajahmundry itself by earning around 10 lakhs per annum and if we calculate this for 35 years the total sum works out around 3.5 crores plus yearly increase of perquisites like increments and DA Bonus etc. which may lead to fetch around another 2.5 crore. Then imagine how much she would be earning and all her earning belongs to you and your son. Is it not?" By that time you may or may not be alive there to calculate the currency you get from both your daughter.

Then Koteeswara Rao got convinced to his audit analysis. He said OK. Then Venkat said"Thanks uncle for affectionate affidavit. All three marriages would take place at a time."

While leaving Koteeswara Rao, he said that I am driving to meet Sri. Ramanna Chaudhary also at Dhavaleshwaram. He dialed Choudhry to convey his presence. Choudhry responded to Venkat's call and said what is the matter Mr. Hero, what made to meet me? Do you require any amount?"

" No uncle, I don't want any money but I have to discuss about the marriage of your elder son Ajay and that made me to meet you immediately, since just few hours back I met your obedient son and he said take a permission before taking my decision to get married with that Durga"

" Please come to Flat No. Rainbow Heights, Morampudi road, as I have shifted my headquarters from Dhavaleshwaram to Rajahmundry. Please come early as I have to go to Income Tax Office to submit Tax Returns."

Venkat said "Oh No only 5minutes. I am almost near your office premises, I am ready to appear before you within seconds."

He parked his car near the Parking place and moved through Lift and knocked alarming bell.

"From inside a hefty noise is heard by murmuring "Come in I am here sitting."

Venkat jumped inside instantly, wished him, took his chair by sitting there and said "I have a very important matter to take consent with you".

"Normally I do not consider any matter important except Money. Any way having come over here to meet me personally, it must be some important matter of purchasing or clearing of loan etc. Is it not?" Said Chaudhary.

"No not any loan, but alliance for your son

Ajay?" Recited Venkat

"Which alliance and what alliance, Are you mad? We are Kammas, we have a High profile both socially, politically, economically and demographically. We are Rulers, Bussiness Tycoons and Large Scale Builders that community is Kamma. Any way please tell me who the hell that party is? Are they Kammas, having high status, standards and wealthy" Come on speak the details early. "Articulated in Hyper voice.

"No Sir, It is Brahmin Community. Not so poor not tycoons but a middleclass community. Perhaps you must have heard about Ramanujam Garu, native of our village, and the alliance is with your son Ajay for his third Daughter Durga." Murmured Venkat.

Choudhary said "What Daughter of that arrogant Brahmin, Ramanujam. What is that he has? Only powder pockets, Churnams and Bhasmas and nothing else."

Venkat communicated that" No Sir. It is not like that. We marry normally to a girl who is fair and good looking fair physically and sincere and honest psychologically. What more you need sir? Regarding weightage of wealth, she would shortly get prestigious Job both in Government service or Private Sector and her salary may more than 16 laksh per year and for 35 years it tent amounts to 4 to 5 crores. What more you want. She hails from highly reputed class, an educated and sincere both in her looks and books.

"Wow! Good calculation. I appreciate your talent. You are most suited for that Appreciation certificate that you received through the District collectors hands. Though you belong to Scheduled caste, you discarded your entitled reservation. Good keep it up. From my side I am Ok. You better have a discussion with my son Ajay as he is the final judge to decide his life partner. I am not coming in his way. It is his life and he need to decide how best he live. In our community there is no binding amongst our family members. We have at liberty to take decision individually. I therefore request to see and decide. Okay." Finally he declared his Judgment to accept Durga as his daughter in law. Venkat felt happy for that and also he became a jubilant one for the clearance of his commitment to settle the marriage of other sisters and then Lakshmi would be ready get married in the same function hall and same auspicious time.

He rushed to his uncle's house to convey the message, but that time Mr. Seetha Ram had come sitting in the drawing room and sipping the tea served by Uoormila. Each of them met and wished for having taking strain in providing shelter to his sisters since it was his duty to take care of them.

It was 5'O clock of the evening. All of sudden all the three sisters dropped down from Auto and wished his brother soon after they see him with Venkat. After taking afternoon breakfast at 5 or so and gone up to the pent house and started discussing about the event that took place after departure to Vizaq. Seetha Ram asked his sisters "why you left the house and came over all the way to Rajahmundry and landing in unknown person's house." Then Venkat clarified that "It was so because they imparted their studies of Junior and Degree colleges and this provision is not available in Dhavaleshwaram. That is all. Seetha Ram left to his in laws and invited them to come along with him. But they said, "No not now, but for next time they would consider"

Seetha Ram smelt that something fishy has taken place in the Village and hence they would compelled to take shelter in Rajahmundry. This was all due the demise of his mother. But he was informed that she died a natural death. Even then his heart failed to accept their theory. Any way he decided to move for the time being and later he can detect the factual position that would have happened. He realized that his sisters must be innocent and frank in dealing with any odds that comes in between them. At the same time father also is not so violent to ask them to decamp from the house for any feud matters.

Thus the cycle of earth took another rotation

around the sun and moved to another new year. Old calendars were thrown in dustbin and new calendar appeared on the wall to indicate that New Year has come up and take over charge in resolving pending issues. The pending issues are the marriages of the Tridevis. In the New Year third sister Durga Declared as Topper in the State Group I examination conducted by Andhra Pradesh Public Service Commission posted as Revenue Divisional Officer, EastGodavariCollectorate at Rajahmundry.

The three Devis proved their metal in spite of so many hurdles and obstacles. Such was the ability of those Trios. They would have lived as spotless life as on date except the smudge of spoiled virginity tagged by their own father. It is all the whirl of spate they had to have on their virtuous life. They prayed their unknown god, the Super Power or the Nuclei to spare them at least for future life so that they can erase those dark spots, and dark titles. Of course time is the strong annihilators that wipe out all the pains and sufferings of past life.

Venkat also has completed his Ph.D. in economics and now qualified to obtain the status of Principal in the same college.Uoormila and her husband Kondiah are now turned more humane than earlier. Similarly the case is the same with Koteeswara Rao, Ramanna Choudhary realized their short falls and now they became more Philanthropist that. Now they are in vanaptasthathey started practicing Swamy Ayyappa Puja discarding all materialistic and mundane desires.

But Ramanujam, is still remained in the same creed and he is after that three asrama of W's (Wealth Women and Wine) though he hails from Brahman community who are supposed to have mastered Brahman knowledge.

According to four stages of ashramswas to lead his lifetime in four states. Ashram (Sanskrit asrama (Devanagiri) in Hinduism. And the stages that include:

"(i) **Brahmacharya:** This stage is the first one and it begins at the age of 20 and extends up to 25 years. In this stages man leads the life of students and practices celibacy. The motto of this life is train to be disciplined himself without crazing for sex.

(ii) **Grihastha:** At this point of time man needs to pay heed to his social and family life. This phase begins from 25 and lasts till 60 years. Grihastha is a crucial stage in one's life where man has to balance both his familial and societal duties. He has to discharge duties of son, brother husband, father and a member of the community.

(iii) **Vanasptsta:** This is the step to partial renunciation the stage ushers in the life of man at an age of 50 and last till 74 years.His children grows up and slowly moves away for the material ties. It is his age for retirement and starts walking a path that will lead to the Divine.

(iv) Sanyasa: The last stage in his life comes when he completely snaps off his worldly ties. This phase begins at 74 and last till he dies. Then he is completely free from the emotional bondage and attachment. He becomes an ascetic. A true devotee is he who knows his duties and fulfills them. Society needs both kind of people who abandons off to pursue God and he who stays within a Social institution and strikes a balance between Karma and Dharma. Now our Ramanujam, being a Brahmin should have a knowledge of these stage and should have practiced this kind of Asramas

On the selection of Durga as Revenue Divisional Officer, through Group I A.P Public Service Examination, all t he trios including Venkat and Kondiah's family became exuberant and exited and started congratulating her. Lakshmi became so happy that there are no boundaries for her cheers. All of the trios forgot their past life which phased out as heinously as possible. Now in their faces one can find a bitter majesty and nobility. They started congratulating her for her success in her career. Venkat said "See our Durga Matha showed her Shakti and remained top on the three Gods Vishnu, Brahma and Eswara. Do you agree Durga?" No uncle, why joking. I have been in touch with General Knowledge and General awareness of the life while studying my B.Sc. It is all God's blessing. That is it."

Kondiah proudly said that "See my daughter has proved her raw diamond into refined and dazzling diamond. I am really proud of my Prince. Do you agree" Then Durga with full of tears filled eyes, prostrated and touched his feet and said "You are the Real God for me, without whose grace and blessing I would not have reached this position." She also said where is my mother goddess Aunty, No, sorry mother aunty I am much indebted to her for enormous fondness she showed to us all along the period we stayed here.

She is none other than Mother Mary! "She touched her feet with much reverence and devotion. For that Uoormila flooded out her tears from her sacred eyes and paid salutation to her act of in-depth devotions that all her three children do survive with happy and wellbeing ness. A Happy and heartwarming occasion. At this point of exchange of emotional tears among parents and daughters, Venkat said loudly"

Please stop your tears so that I may be drowned in the floods of your tears and attain Mukti without marriage, the Grihastasrama. On this occasion I have decided to take you all to Anand Regency for dinner. Right. I have never seen such Triveni sangam in life which is more sacred than the Ganga Yamuna and Saraswathi Sangam. So this is my small "Anjali" being presented by going to Anand Regency and have dinner there."

On hearing the news of Durga's selection as RDO, number of neighboring residents came and wished mainly to Uoormila and Kondiah who are their foster Father and Mother. They said "We proudly say that all the Dieties like Indra, Vishnu, Brahma and Trimurthy from the heaven, must have sprinkled the showers of their blessings on this Ideal family." While going back to their respective houses, the colony members announced proudly that "We the Society Members wanted to arrange grand reception to facilitate the occasion. Hence all of you kindly go over tour community Hall on Sunday that is day after tomorrow which is day Navarathri. You people also call on your relatives and friends on this day. We shall handover a set of printed invitation cards by evening today. Okay"

Venkat and party cruised out to Anand Regency by 7'O' clock.Lakshmi and sisters with Venkat and foster parents had very posh and delicious dinner where in both vegetarian and Non-vegetarian is arranged since Venkat knows well that the three Sisters hesitate to touch Non-veg food. Uoormila also did not cook Non-Veg food during their stay all along six years. That is the sacrifice that required and not the sacrifice that most of Muslims do in the name of Idul Adha-Festival of Sacrifice, which also called Bakrid- sacrificing a goat. The sacrifice that Venkat made by discarding himself Reserved Candidature is also a real sacrifice far greater than any other sacrifice except committing suicide to keep their word.

Lakshmi passed on the news of Selection of Durga for the post of RDO, to Seetha Ram. He also felt happy and promised to come to Visit Rajahmundry on Sunday along with his family. Lakshmi also informed to Koteeswara Rao, Ramanna Choudhary Chiranjeevi and Ajay about the news of Durga's selection as RDO and reception on Sunday.

SCENE 8

VILLIAN PROVED PHILISTINE AND PEDOPHILE TRIOS CRUSHED

Lakshmi while searching old valet, she noticed one a bunch of 4 pages duly written something therein. She questioned "What is this letter? Who gave it me?"

She took it andstarted reading wherein it was addressed to her that"My dear Princes Lakshmi"……Now she could recollect that it was the letter of "my mother who gave it to me before her death. Oh No I am sorry mom"

She took her chair at her table and started reading the letter where in it was written by her mother that " MY dear Lakshmi, as you are elder and grown one I am addressing to you. Why I was compelled a letter to you because I could face you and tell your about your father's sexual atrocities.

Your grandfather who named as Rangacharya, a noted Ayurvedic Physician in Peddapuram. He was so famous that everybody in entire Konaseema and Vizaq, knew him as great Social reformer and Ayurvedic expert. He was bachelor then. On seeing him my father (that is your grandfather) Yoganand who is also equally famous for his writing of Novels,

Poems, and Panchangam etc. approached him for my marriage with his son Ramanujam. Of course I had four other sisters and two brothers. Then I was so beautiful that I used to be called as Vennela (Moon light). Your father on seeing me must have fall flat and immediately accepted our proposal without any formalities of Katnam of giving gold and other furniture set that are normally given by the bride party to groom. I was also fallen in love with him by his good looking personality. And within three months our marriage was performed. In the beginning he was looking most moderate and well-mannered personality. He had very good hold in Vedas translations and interpretations."

Your father always feeling of high ofhim and he maintained silence in talking with our sisters, brothers. When he talks, he appeared that used to talk with every word with weight and measurement. I used to Joke him "Did you work any time in the Department of Weights and Measurement?" For that small petty joke he used to hit me and due that with entire pleasant mood used to be shelved down in the water. Day after day he used keep me in distance. I could not notice as to why he is keeping distance with me. I was questioning myself "Has my beauty is slipping down? Any mistake from side? Am I not preparing good dishes?" Like that I used to think and the answer I found was not at all proved negative. Why he is disliking me as he was on first two nights of our marriage. Nothing happened as far as my knowledge goes? Then why?

Then I called my father secretly and explained my position. My father said "perhaps he must be crazy for dowry" Then he contacted him directly and said "My son, do you requireany dowry, and if it is so please inform so that I can arrange for gold and cash within my capacity." But he replied no Uncle. I am not interested. But if you feel so kindly ask my father and not to me. We both wife and husband are doing well.

For that he got delighted very much and asked both of to attend his house in the evening and spend three nights as it is a formality also in our tradition. Finally your father felt happy and we went there and stayed there.

Next day morning one of your aunt complained me that "she is feeling "drowsy and nostalgic". She also said that her entire body is filled with gum type stains. And next day another aunt said the same thing. She was minor one. Third day another your younger aunt also complained of the same problem.

It was all suspense. Nothing could be detected. The matter was subsided. After another month later we went to our house for attending to the reception of my brother's marriage at Anakapalli, your grandmother also faced the same tragedy. Though yourgrandmother is name sake is grandmother but she was looking smart, and hence she was targeted to rape by somebody. All these incidents caused us dirty and ugly to discuss with each other. Your grandmother told me in personal that "during our stay t at Anakapalli somebody came to me and raped me like a monster, I didn't know who that bastard was." But her matter also was kept as secret as the news may spoil the relationship of with each other in our family and marriages of young generations would not take place if once it is unearthed.

Analogously, time passed, but one day your brother's daughter Bujji, who was aged 4 or so was playing in corridor of 1st floor, Your father seems to have embraced her and started penetrating of his penis and on account of pain she was crying. But even then he did not leave her and finally he released his semen inside her small vagina. After seeing this agility I took one big stick lying there on upstairs and hit number times that I did not know how many. Luckily I was the only person who witnessed this atrocity. Many other family members also came to me on the first floor to enquire about the mishap. But I convinced them that the baby was crying on seeing the monkey.

But my sisters who were raped by your father became pregnant and I could handle the situation by convincing them by telling that "it was factor of indigestion not more than that". Thus I could put my parents calm. I took my sisters to the hospital and aborted them without anybody's knowledge. I convincedmy sisters also that if we openly say that your pregnancy without marriage will lead many complications and, their fate would be on stake hence I advised them not to make much hue and cry otherwise our family's prestige would be thrown on roads and your life also will be condemned and they remain unmarried till the end of their life. Hence they could calm down. It is almost synonymous with your case.

That was the dirty thing happened in my parents' home and in my family life and hence I have decided to leave the world without making any further noise. So you please decide as favorably as possible.

I pray God to save you all from the clutches of that monster. With wishes.

Yours Affectionately

Saraswathi

While noting all the events ascribed by her mother"that her father ruined the life teenaged girls of his own relatives and daughters" she decided to kill him but she could control her fury and decided to keep pending for the time being. Now she called on Venkat to discuss about the marriage of her sisters along with herself.

Venkat promptly present before her love partner. Venkat said in detail about the consultations with both Koteeswara Rao and Choudhry and the result is both ready for the alliance, since it is related to Sri Ramanujam most gentle revered person in the village.

Then Lakshmi told him" to fix the date and see that all the three marriages takes place in a single stroke."

Instantly said by Venkat that, " How is it possible? Your sister Durga is undertraining until three months. Then what?"

Lakshmi said "Yes, I have forgotten. Meanwhile let us consult the Panthulu garu about proper propitious day in the month of June. Right!"

"Tomorrow any how we are all celebrating the occasion of Durga's selection as RDO. We would consult him to come here for the consultation. Right" stated by Venkat.

"OK Boss. I do accept your sincere advice. Our Brother is also coming let us utilize his services in this regard, since he is the elder person from our side." Said Lakshmi

"Yes Madam. Your order is authority to follow. That is it? "Said Venkat

Lakshmi gave kiss to Venkat and he roamed in the fairy land for just minute and felt high of himself and desired to chatter on Public meeting that" He is the most Smart and Top Notch in the world"

On Sunday morning the grand occasion of reception arranged by the Padmavathi Nagar Society in their community Hall. Venkat gave a lecture on Societies development on cooperative basis and their achievements, in his inaugural speech.

Then Lakshmi stated that" this Society consists of members who always much sought after the development and progress of this society. All the members are equally moved together, acting all as a unit to tackle any problems that they face across while living as society member. She said" I mean that irrespective their caste, creed, community or status have joined in any activity that related to welfare of the society. This made me to appreciate all the members of the society. I therefore convey my in depth gratitude and salute to you all, Thank You."

Finally Durga, the chief guest, started saying that" I acknowledge with many thanks to the all the society member for having made me a VIP of this reception. Here in this connection I want give small and precise speech, provided you all jointly permitted"

Almost all the members said Right, "You please proceed in giving your view on any social burning issue that we could know better than we have been brought up under certain set of tradition."

Then she said thanks all the member and said "I would like to give a brief speech on the "The Nationalism and casteism" which is nothing but a most burning issue that has become an obstacle for better development of ourselves andof our country. We are unable to call this country as our mother Nation since the problem is not only related to this region or that community but related entire India. The entire people recognize us what a great people we are?"

Before coming to our objective theme Casteism" I would like to give a brief picture of our Mother India and the result of the picture would become a suitable answer for Casteism?

Here those who have attended, must be more qualified and more well versed about the History and other cultural facts Even then I would like bring forth certain facts that I have collected from my reading of Books on India and its' glory . Our India is called cradle of human race, the birth place of human speech, the mother of History, the grandmother of Legends and great grandmother of traditions our most valuable and most instructive materials in the in history of man are treasured up in India only. If I were asked under what sky the human mind has most fully developed some of its choicest gifts has most deeply pondered on the greatest of life and has found solution, I should point out India.

Such was our India's incredibility. Our India and our Indian Culture has an extraordinary impact over the world ? The Indian culture labeled as an amalgamation of several cultures, spans across the Indian sub-continent and has been influenced by history that is several millennia old. Many elements India's culture such as Indian Religions, Indian Philosophy and Indian culture have profound impact across the world. One great Historian and Scholar from America has stated that " India is the sixth largest country in the world, largest democracy ever practiced by man on this planet and one of the most ancient and living civilization will capture her ancient number one place in World as the richest nation and economic giant on Earth in the 21st Century.

Let me bring forth the realm of remembrance of our members that is how our India or Indian is being clapped with emotional tears on witnessing the immortal achievements by our great India. We have

Decimal system long before 2000 years even earlier period of 6000 years, the idea of Zero; Numerical Notations; Fibonacci Numbers; Binary numbers; Algorithms; Algebra; Ruler Measurement like scale; Theory of Atom proposed by Kanada; Heliocentric theory invented by Aryabhatta; Woot Steel; Seamless Meta Globe; Plastic Surgery called Rhinoplasty by ancient Ayurvedic sages; Cataract Surgery; Ayurveda; Iron cased Rockets; Theory of Evolution through Dasavathara; Age of Universe as 4 trillion years quoted in Rig-Veda; Iron Pillar of Asoka in Delhi (black smithy); Step wells; Stupa; Flush out toilets used in Mohenjo-Daro-Harappa of Indus Valley Civilization 3rd Millennium; Shampoo; Gravity; Raman Effect; First and oldest University in the World called Taxila in 700BC ; Algebra with 10 to the power of 50; India was the only source of Diamonds and spices in the Universe; Sushrutha (Surgery) 2000 years back and Grammar around 5000 years back

Wheeler Wilcox World's famous Historian and Writer stated that 'India the land of Vedas the remarkable works contain notably religious ideas for perfect life but also facts which Science has proven true electricity, radium Electronics, Air ship, all were known to the Seers who founded Vedas.

To be in brief nothing has left undone either man or nature to make the most extraordinary country that the Sun visits on his rounds. Nothing seem to have been forgotten, nothing overlooked by Vedic India. Besides this rich investments and discoveries, the spoken written language by seers and Vedas, was the Sanskrit whatever be its antiquity is a wonderful structure, more perfect than the Greek more copious than the Latin and more exquisitely refined than either. In this connection French Philosopher Romaine Rollin states if there is one place on the face of Earth where all the dreams of living man have found home from very earliest days when man began the dream of existence that is Land of India. He also stated that India has very advanced technology in terms of Hindu Astronauts in around 6000 BCE. Vedas contain an account of the dimensions of Earth, sun, Moon and Galaxies calendar and Constellations.

Again Will Durant, an American Historian and Writer finally said: India was the mother land of our civilized human race, and Sanskrit the mother of Europe's language, she was the mother of our Philosophy, Mother of much of mathematics, Mother through village community of local self-Governments and Democracy (Panchayathi Raj system), and thus Mother India is Mother of us all.

The glory of India was totally eclipsed by the foreign invaders right from the Alexander, Musllius to the British colonists. It may be called as Dark Age of India for the past one millennium. To bring back our Mother India's greatness and glory, it became our duty the post Indian-Independence generation to discard, casteism, racism, communalism, that has become an interruption for the growth and development of Mother India and development Nationalism.

Though the word Nationalism looks superfluous in the Age of Globalization, but in my view it is necessary for those who have been in particular space that is geographically bounded with. We owe very much to our land called home and that home land becomes patent right to live as a member of that society and that space becomes our Mother land. It is therefore it becomes one's creed or political ideology that involves an individual identifying with or becoming attached to one's nation. Nationalism generates Patriotism which is an essential core of existence in that Nation. Whenever our Nation face the threat of invasion from the foreigners that demands confrontation. The real Patriotism is arsenal to meet the challenge and counter ride it.

The advent of nationalism results to the birth of Patriotism. If it is lacking at the time of intrusions we will become Slaves of the foreigners and live with fear and tear. Our life will survive on the gesture of the foreigners as had been we underwent since thousands of years. At this juncture I would recall the saying that "He who lost his patriotic spirit has lost himself and whole world forget about him". We will be losing our identity. If anybody question who are? Where from you have come? Then our answer would be nothing more than Zero. That is the importance of nationalism. It is therefore we being related to nation India should get United. If you still go on thinking that I am a Brahmin My duty is to pray and perform rituals of God. Kshatriya says I when Brahmins is not cooperating the stage of alarm, why should I go and fight and likewise all castes will have their agonies and importance and hence they fail to challenge the situation. Finally we have to lose our identity and act like Slaves. Do you want see that our history repeated again and again."

According to Rig Veda hymn, the different classes sprang from four limbs of the Creator, Brahma. The creators Mouth became the Brahman priests, his two arms formed the Rajanya (Kshatriya) the warriors and Kings, his two thighs formed the Vaishya, who are assigned to look after Land and bussiness, and from his were born the Sudra (untouchable) artisans and servants. It was meant to show that the four classes stood in relations to the social organs of the primordial Man to his body. Together they had to function to give vitality to the body of politic.

However in Bhagavad Gita, on the four fold divisions of castes, say the creator "created by according to apportionment of qualities and duties not by birth not sacrament not by learning make one Dvija (twice-born) but righteous conduct alone cause it. Be he a Sudra, or a member of any other class say the Lord in the same epic "He that serves as raft on raffles current or helps to ford the unfordable deserves respect in every way."

This CASTE System became fixed and hereditary with the emergence of Hinduism and its beliefs of pollution and rebirth. The Laws of Manu (Manusmruthi) refers to impurity and servility of that caste, while affirming the dominance and total impurity of Brahmins. Those form the "Lowest Caste are to that their place in the caste hierarchy is due to their sins inpast life. Vivid punishments of torture and death are assigned for crimes such as gaining literacy or insulting member of a dominant caste. Among the writings of Hindu religious texts, the Manusmruthi is undoubtedly the most authoritative one, legitimating social exclusion and introducing absolute inequality as the guiding principle of social relations.

Thus there is no authoritative and solid sayings is there in our epics or Vedas or even Upanishads that the Caste system is not authenticated. In my opinion. As a human of common sense the caste system affects the society by making people more exposed to prejudice, stereotyping andother things. These differences in ranking often cause disputes with in the society. It is obvious to state that how its effects the society depends on how you see it. Thus there is no point in calling a system or a process rather it is an evil. Indian society is caste ridden. This division of society into so many religions castes and sub-casts comes in the way of Unity and integrity of the Indian nation. People vote on basis of caste and religion and do not take the merits of the candidates into consideration. Democracy itself has become a mockery owing to this evil.

It is here I am to say that "the caste system cannot be eradicated without changing the mindset of the people, since the very caste system itself is a social evil. Casteism proved that it is humanly cre-ated tradition and not God related revelation. Even Gandhi, the so called Mahatma, himself did not mo-bilize a movement for the eradication of untouch-ability. He could say only that all Untouchables are Harijans and all Mlechhas are Girijans. That is again a foolish attribution of addressing like that way to the humans in general. Here Hari means God, and if that God is called to be perfect Atman, he could not have created imperfect being. Hence his theory is illogical and unacceptable. Vyasa Muni, Valmiki, Va-sichta, almost a Munis who are learned and became great souls though they are by birth Sudras. So this type of categorization is rubbish.

I therefore state that if the evil of casteism ought to be eradicated and every possible efforts should be made to educate the people thus create a strong public opinion against this evilslike untouchability, diversity, lack of social thinking, failure of Democracy (Human is One) woman slavery and communal violence. Democracy declared that all are free, to vote, claim justice andmove as one Human. And this democracy facing crunch and carrying can of worms.

You just bestow your attention on the functioning of this Padma Nagar society, where all the residents of the society are called members and every member may be related different communities, like be Muslim, Brahmin, Sudra, Christian or Tribal are even Harijans. Despite of the compartments, all of them are treated as a Member of society and whenever they gather for discuss any matter relating to society is being discussed with universalityand solidarity. Let me conclude my speechon Casteism by transmitting few steps to be taken to eradicate casteism. The first and foremost formula of eradication is "Inter caste Marriage" and second one is "Fight against Reservation system and cooperate with the Government to have common platform of "common economic policy and Unitary stand while adopting development program.

You see the example of our society member sitting here as chair person. You know what an awesome deed he has done is "he has discarded his name from the List of Reservation and relinquished the benefits of Reservation. He has requested to the Government to delete his candidature from the list of Reservation". Further I can give few   more references and they are none than Mr. Seetha Ram, being Brahmin he married Sudra community girl, Mr. Chiranjeevi, being a Sudra he is going to marry Brahmin girl whois none other than Saraswathi and myself   is going to marry Mr. Ajay from Sudra Community. One more person is ignored here and she is my elder sister Lakshmi is marrying with Venkat who is Harijan by birth."

"Thus I conclude my speech with a request to think of my speech and try to cooperate with the government as a basic unit. On concluding her speech almost all the members presented on the occasion became spell bounded for her voracious lecture and acquainted with in-depth knowledge of India's social structure and its glory. They surrounded and crowned her with garlands.

Thank you all the members of the society for having given an opportunity to talk with you all. With good wishes to you all. Soon after finishing her lecture many members engulfed her with garlands and took snaps with her and promised her that they would certainly follow her footsteps.

Finally Venkat gave a concluding speech amongst claps and shouting with thanks as Mr. Hero of East Godavari District. He further announced that" their intercast marriage would become example of exemplary act and these marriages are going to be celebrated on Next Sunday. So kindly treat that they are being performed in your houses and see that they are all blessed with your love and affection therewith. Thank You.

Venkat started wishing all the three daughters in achieving the best career in their life without the help of their parents. Seetha Ram also congratulated both his sisters and Venkat for the efforts jointly for attaining his sisters their goals.

But even now Seetha Ram still doubting why his father is not free to visit this occasion. Had they informed to him he would have certainly paid visit and blessed them. Now the question arises as to why he was not invited to this function? It appears to him as mystery. He wanted to chase it and know what is what? Who is right and who is wrong?

However, he could not control his anxiety and wanted to derive exact information from Lakshmi and Venkat about his fathers' absence. He called on both Venkat and Lakshmi to the Guest room, an exclusive room meant for Guests.

On their arrival, Seetha Ram asked bluntly why and what is the matter for not inviting our father here on this celebration. Lakshmi said "My dear brother there is much ado about him to which I shall let you know later. It is better to avoid discussing about him at this juncture.

However she asked to Venkat to "move out for a while so that some important topic need to be discussed with my brother. I am sorry for keeping out from this secret discussion"

The movement Venkat left the room, Lakshmi enquired with Seetha Ram by asking that" Have you ever been to Village after your marriage, along with your family"

In response to her question, Seetha Ram said "Yes we had been to Dhavaleshwaram both myself and Radhika just after sixth moths of our marriage"

She said again "Did you stay there? If so how many days you stayed there?

He said "I think we stayed there in our house for about two days and third day we left to Visakhapatnam. Why you ask me like that? It is our house I can go there and stay there as long as I want to do so. Any objection? We are all brought up and there only. What is that strange in our staying there?"

"My dear brother. Don't think otherwise. There is nothing wrong in going there to our house and stay there. The situation is more different now. You and your wife had been there. Is isn't? That is the difference. Any way I don't want to discuss in this matter? You would learn soon about the things that happened there?"

" What is that you are telling? Are there any Devils roaming inside our house? You questions looks strange for me." Said Seetha Ram."

"Did our Vadina felt strange while getting awakened from the bed next day in the morning?" She further questioned.

For that question Seetha Ram Stumbled and said "How could you know about her feeling of drowsiness on the next day morning? I am unable understand. Father told her to take some powder to which he gave for her gynecological ailment and he declared she would be alright within a month and she will be blessed with child. That is it. What is this all this non-sense questions you are asking me all the way? I am unable to understand? That is our house and he is our father and none else He is not a demon worshipper for your information."

All of a sudden Venkat said loudly "Oh dear Ram your father has come and see he is asking you and your family?"

"See my father has visited us and let us meet him" Said.

Lakshmi said "you go first and I will be joining with shortly" The moment he left , Lakshmi asked Seetha Ram to go to market and get one CCTV camera and fix it on the first floor or near the corridor of the entrance"

"Why so urgent Madam. Why that camera now here in we are all here how can anyone can come and loot anything and escape from here?" asked Venkat with much honestly.

Lakshmi said "Right occasion seems to have come? Let us utilize it and show the public how cruel my father is? Time has come to punish him let my life be spoiled. My sisters would be safe is it not?"

Venkat said "No don't take such radical step now itself. Let us wait and watch?"

"Now I am unable to bear this mental strain. Let me bring forth the secret out. This is a peculiar situation that no daughter will face such ghastly situation that me including my sisters endured all the way. I   cannot face the questions being put forth by society all along There is no matter if die in this strange war between father and daughter. One day or other the secret need to be unearthed. What do you say? Kindly cooperate with me and pardon me also if lose my life in the combat?"

Venkat said "Why do you take law into your hand? Leave him to his fate. God will punish him at any cost. My sincere advice is don't get furious at this juncture? You think of your life and your two sister's life which will be stanchioned"

Then Lakshmi said" See Venkat don't block me? See on account of all the lives of my sisters, brothers and his children' is getting betted in the fame gambling being played by that dirty maniac. You know that my mother died abruptly, myself and my sisters were faced his torture and he would play with my brother's life. I am any way lost my credibility and passing on my time with unsurpassable agony. I want put an end and put Full Stop to this burning issue. One more thing kindly bring one trident either from some temple or from the shop, if you don't mind"

Venkat viewed the situation and felt it as Just. But.........any way I shall arrange both CCTV and Camera and Trident.....Oh god Save my beloved Lakshmi please." By going murmuring about God he went to the market and secure all the items she invoiced and fixed and placed them in the assigned places as per Lakshmi's wish.

Both Durga and Saraswathi could watch the scene right from the beginning by hiding behind the main door. They too decided to cooperate with her sister and they too could hired the Trident from nearby Temple by paying some ransom to the Pujari.

On other side Seetha Ram went to Hall and prostrated to touch his feet of his father Ramanujam and enquired about his welfare. They went to Radhika and asked her to show our baby Jyothi who is no running 4. Ramanujam took her and lifted her at his chest and started kissing and blessing. Radhika said "Uncle I got this child with your blessing and the medicine you gave for me. Please bless me."

"He immediately said by placing his hand on her head chanted as: Ayushmanbhava" (Long live)"

He hugged her with much longing. The moment he touched her all of a sudden she took back and ran away from there. Seetha Ram also went after her and asked her "What is the matter" Just now you were all right and all of a sudden you raced out why?" She said nothing. It is OK. Seetha Ram said"

My father is not a stranger he is your father also is it not?"

She said "Yes" with running tears from her eyes?

She again raced out from there and started searching for Lakshmi and others and they found nowhere and hence she took rickshaw and went to parent's house.

Why she escaped from there a Big Question" Let us wait for some time to learn about the shock she faced"

While embracing her, his father in law seems to have erectedhis cock to touch her pussy which is behind the saree and her inner.This made her to recall the earlier experience she had in his father in laws house. Same type of hug, smell and muscles. Now she grasped that it is none other than his own father in law who fucked her all over the night by giving some sedative medicine while sleeping in the night when she went along with Seetha Ram 5 years back. Oh my God what a crook that fellow is?"

That was the reason why she ran away from there to her mother's houseasked her Mummy to give a glass of water and on receiving it from her mother to drink nearly three tumblers of water one after another and her entire body became wet with sweating. Her mother asked " Why are you shiver-ing? Why this sweating? Have seen any dangerous snake any way around that colony? Or any witch--breeze you noticed? What is the matter my dear, tell me. She said "Mummy give me a rug so that I can sleep in warmth for a while. Don't disturb Please?"

Okay I don't disturb you by posing questions.

Take rest as long as you can. I shall get hot coffee. Right?

"Mummy not now after an hour please? It seems Radhika mind is not in her control. She is unable to decide whether to tell her about his nasty act or not? What to do and what to reply to her mother's questions and likewise she slept in deep sleep.She forgotbring her daughter along with her who was playing with Seetha Ram.

Soon after getting up she recollected about her daughter and hence she got up from the bed and moved back to Seetha Ram. There at Venkat's aunt's house she looked playing with some children of the colony. Then her palpitation of heart beating came and calm down.

As Lakshmi was present there she could grasp the situation and estimated what actually would have happened Radhika during her visit to their village and their house. She again got wild on calculating the event how methodically she would have been raped by her father, Ramanujam.

She said in herself "she is also has fallen prey to this Monster". She wanted move and hit him with some rod noticed nearby but occasion is not in her favor. She thought "that right occasion would be when she seize him red handled with full-fledged evidence. I do not care in capturing him and kill him with trident. That would be only punishment that she can give to him so that many innocent girls would not fall prey to that beast"

After few minutes Venkat came with all the equipment she prescribed to bring. She requested to fix these items except the trident on the corroded adjacent to the door where beds are spread for the guests to sleep and where Ramanujam also may come to take rest. She knew pretty well that he would be one of three guests who would be visiting from outside the city and they are Seetha Ram, Radhika and Ramanujam.

As it was the day of Durga Puja, all most all ladies assembled in the ground floor. And the chief role of Kalimatha to be taken by Durga her sister. This occasion of Puja became right background for the act they wanted to execute. Having known that on this puja occasion Ramanujam would be joining with them since she had asked Venkat to send a special invitation card to her father a fortnight earlier.

Most of the colony members and out guests who gathered there started singing songs praising v Goddess Matha. She killed all the demons to whom the Tri Devas failed to do so, it is so because she is considered as the Great Power, the Great Nuclei of the universe. She possess great valor and courage to kill hard core demons on Earth. She is also considered as the Original Shakti or Adi ParaSalthi, as per Hindu Mythology. It is she who gave birth to three Devas viz. Vishnu, Brahma and Shiva. She is like Mother Nature and always carry Trident with her for hunting the Demons who used to Put off Fire arranged by the seers to Perform Yagna by chanting tenets of Rig-Veda a (ritual to offer Super God) in the name of Yagna (a ritual of sacrifice).

Venkat thought that "How can such an elderly person do commit rape amongst the heavy crowd sleeping in the house? It would be a waste of energy. Hence thought better to go to second floor and submerged in deep sleep with a cool breeze fanning in around him.

After prayer is over, all the guests and society members took dinner and moved to their respective places for sleep. Seetha Ram and his family tried to move to his in laws house but out of obligation they decided to stay in the Kondia's house itself. Though Radhika is not in favor of sleeping here as her father in law is also staying there. But out of her husband's pressure she stayed and decided to sleep in the hall along with other ladies. Seetha Ram and his child slept near veranda where cool breeze is blowing.

It was almost midnight and all of a sudden Ramanujam who acted as sleeping in deep sleep woke up and took the child nearby open place where nobody seen sleeping and started to open the child's gown and kissing entire body particular at the central point that is the pussy with great raze. He did not know he is being shot in camera and all images are being recorded in the CCTV besides the observation of six eyes with a blaze of anger. Without noticing all these things, Ramanujam started inserting his cock inthat child's pussy as if he found a diamond in his hands.Though baby is crying he could control himself and continued his nasty act by pressing her mouth.

Then Durga took her trident and rushed to the spot to kill that Psycho. Behind her Lakshmi and Saraswathi followed and raised their tridents and hit directly to his cock and testes. Likewise one after anothertridentsfollowed and smashed that trio spot and smashed the entirecentral point of Ramanjam's body. And with this he shouted in pitch and roared like a wounded tiger. With this roaring shouts all the members got up including Seetha Ram and saw his father's position and carried his body on the shoulders and went down and taken to nearby Hospital?

Then all the three Sisters carried the blood soaked Tridents down to the ground and moved themselves to nearest Police Station gave a statement that "We Trios have killed our father" The Police Inspector Veera Bhadriah who was on Duty then. He recorded all the statements given by the Three Sisters and took them under custody.

Here Venkat is in dizzy mood and went down to see the happening. Again he went up to the Varanda where the TV record and Camera collected them and handed over to the police station for their perusal.

The moment Ramanujam got admitted in the hospital with the help of Seetha Ram, he underwent a major operation and all the tri organs were removed and made the area plain by leaving some hole for passing urine. On the early hours of next day morning he came to his senses and got discharged from the hospital. The hospital bill including diagnosis report with surgery details.

Now Seetha Ram is in a reel of emotions and questions? He questioned himself why our father was attempted to be killed by three of his own daughters? What made them to take such a serious action?

He took his father along with him by engaging an Ambulance and took him to his in-law's house. All the members of his family that is Koteeswara Rao, Aunt and Radhika with their child Jyothi were present there.But Mr. Koteeswara asked Seetha Ram not to bring him inside and take to Dhavaleshwaram and ensured that he stayed there itself. Seetha Ram took him through Ambulance to Dhavaleshwaram.

SCENE 9

MONSTER COURT MARSHALLED

Three days later all the three sisters were taken to court and with the permission granted by the District Judge to keep them in remand in woman police station, they were taken into police station. Later on after week, Court summoned to both parties to attend the court for prosecution.

Seetha Ram engaged an Advocate to fight against the case. The court ordered to appear the in defense of the accused lawyer to submit his defense reply.

Meanwhile all the Tridevis got bail until the court passits judgment.

After number of adjournments the court gave date for cross examining the both Tridevis who attempted to kill him and to the culprit himself. During the cross examination the court came to conclusion that the main culprit is the plaintiff himself on seeing the video recording, the powder he used to make his daughters to drowse and semi –unconscious proved to be a mixture of cocaine and other sedative drugs, prepared by himself.

On confirming his indulgence with series of adultery campaign against his own daughters the Court ordered to get the culprit examined by the Psychiatrist. He was taken to Visakhapatnam where Government approved els, Psychiatrist is available.

On series of examinations and questions he arrived to a conclusion "that the culprit is not a Psycho. His personality is very normal but molestationmust be due to consuming drugs with an intention to commit adultery to any female irrespective of the fact that that female is an adult, teenaged or even child girls whether they are closely related or not. His adamant and deliberate intention is, he is always in search for the chanceto indulge with sexual intercourse. In the past about two years back he had indulged in such acts forgetting the status of opposite person who was his own mother in law and her daughters other than his wife. He initiated in using the steroids prepared by him and uses as an experiment before marketing it. His aim is mainly to earn money by selling his product to the patients or rightly say his consumers to practice same type of illegitimacy. He is not a normal or subnormal personality but abnormal and extrovert in his character. To be in nut shell, he is a cunning fox in this society which is by all means a concrete Jungle. He is also a pedophile in nature which is rare feature in a civilized humans. Thus it can be rightly said that "whatever he did this illicit act by falling prey to the lust irrespective of the social or family relations. Indeed he waits for the chance or occasion for committing rape with deliberate motivation. He is pedophile in character and arrogant in following human values, while carrying his dignity in living civilized society. Besides this he is regular consumer of Drugs preparation and using for self while preparing for adultery"

The Plaintiff counsel quested the Judge "Your Honor, I am inclined to ask few questions to the three sister who mercilessly caused damage to his central part of the body which is also a serious in terms of IPC Act.

The Judge gave permission to do so. The Counselor asked the trio one after another that "why all you kept the matter in secret without resorting to the court for the injustice they faced with their father"

Then Lakshmi said politely that "This matter was related the honor of our family where our father, though, he is culprit, we felt that it was mainly related to the prestige of our father and his family. More so we thought that he grown old and perhaps he would have caused the attempt of atrocity. Moreover, he was the person who brought upus to this level and maintained us. We maintained very good relationship with each other till that incident took place. Hence we all three decided to ignore and condone him. Hence we did not lodge any complaint either with either police or Court or not even to our mother who is elder person to all of us.

First of all we failed to know who exactly that person was who involved with adulteration with ours. We are always suspecting other person other than our family. And when we came to know through the Video we got shocked to resort to Mr. Venkat who was only the well-wisher of me and my sisters. Thus the time was lapsed in confirming the person who would be that Monster. But after knowing that he was our father himself we failed to decide what action need to be taken over?

But we could not tolerate when that dirty man attempted both my sister in law and our brother's daughter who is so innocent and infant in her tender age who can't reasonably.......It is therefore we decided and make public at least now at the juncture of spoiling the innocent child who is only 4 year's old and that too with his granddaughter. We could not tolerate that ghastly and nasty act to be done with such small child.

For that judge said "Yes it was a right decision you have had taken in making public the act of adultery with small child"

The Defense counselor asked to Ramanujam why he acted this way with your offshoots. Did you not feel shame in doing soit is why because a daughter always look up to her father as a shield of her dignity and honor? But in reverse you became a queer of her honor why what makes you to do so? "

Ramanujam said "Yes I do believe. But my argument is what is wrong in using her for my passion when she is my own estate? I sowed a seed and she is born and it becomes my priority to use her. Take the case of Brahma and Saraswathi. The movement Brahma created Saraswathi he fell in lovewith her and finally they became parents of the Universe. That is it. So nothing wrong, in my view."

For his arrogant reply entire members who are present in court, laughed at him and abused him as monster.

Then the Defense Lawyer said it is all stories. If, for a while we consider that they are true, but the same mythology gave a suitable reply in punishing Brahma for his misstate and Lord Shiva took his trident and cut his fifth head which can sight above head. Hence Brahma has only four heads instead of five " He further argued that"See Mr. Ramanujam, in your own Hindu sacred scripts like Manusmruthi it is asserted that in the cases of any atrocities like rape on women, in Hinduism asserts that as agirl she should run and seek protection of her "father", as a young women to her "husband" and as a widow her "son". This Section of Manusmruthi clearly asserts that father, husband and son all are male to protect their relative woman and provide shelter or asylum to be provided by father, husband and son. But whereas you being a father why did you rape, even having a wife with you? Is it not Adharma? When Draupadi in Mahabharata was stripped down with her sarees by Dussasana, then your God Lord Krishna abused and called it asAdharma committed by Bhishmacharya, Kripacharya, Dhritarashtra, Sakuni and other elders of Kauravas who were present in the Court of Duryodhana, for having simply observing the scene stripping of clothes of woman folk instead ofraising any objection or protecting her. And the result was the greatest war of Kurukhsetra was fought in which allthose observers who mainly maintained silence that itself is Adharma' and they were killed by Arjuna and Bhīma in particular and Pandavas in general. See what an importance the woman is considered in our Mythology? They were even considered as Goddesses of wealth, you know?"

For that Ramanujam simply bow down his head and said "sorry. It was my grave mistake. Hence I am ready to face any punishment the court is accorded therewith."

On hearing is statement the lawyers further

stated that "this started to using the Narcotic drugs to assault the minor girls and he used serve it as Medicine to the patients who used to visit him for clinical gesture and to arraign freedom from the diseases like Asthma, Bronchitis and even Tuberculosis, which again attract the provisions of the Narcotic drugs and Psychotropic Substance Act 1984 which is punishable under the Sections of 17 and 225 of the Indian Penal Code. Hence this man need punishment not only under section 497 of violence against woman folk by way of molestation and rape. He is therefore person that requires capital punishment. "With this I rest my Lord"

The lawyer of accused requested the Judge to interrogate the alleged Victims of molestation one after the other. Judge gave permission and asked all the trios, and Radhika.

For that Judge said "where is the need to examine them when the accused himself has accepted that he has done the crime against his daughters and what for they need again to be examination since it would cause damage to the honor of the those girls. Hence No permission please. Such examination requires when the accused refused to accept of the crime. It is a simple matter and subject of common sense."

For that the Plaintiff Lawyer got convinced and said "Sorry My Lord and hence also rests herewith.

Judge took the view of the counsel of plaintiff and passed on the following preamble and final Judgment that includes:

1. On thorough examination and investigation of the Videos twice recorded, and the letter written by the culprits wife Smt. Saraswathi, the statements presented by the Tridevis and the recorded statement of culprits daughter in law that Radhika, and Psychiatrist Report; Court came a decision to pass Judgment which must be said as an Historic Judgment which is read as follows"

It is appalling to see that rape rears its ugly façade almost every one such dark reality in the Indian society that devastate a women's soul, shatters herself respect and for a few purges their hope to live. It shakes the insight of woman once was a "happy Person" and had no clue of being victim of the said horrifying and nightmarish encounters where the daughters had been raped by none else but his own progenitor. A daughter always look up to her father as a shield of her dignity and honor which is an intrinsic facet of a family especially of father(shield for her dignity and honor which is an intrinsic) and daughter relationship is ravaged in such a sordid manner and the Protector becomes the Perpetrator. In such a case the offense assumes a greater degree of vulnerability which shall not go unpunished. There can never a graver heinous crime that the father being charged of raping his own daughter. It is also proved that he was not suffering with any psychological trauma but he was drug addict too.

2. It is an intentional and deliberate with preplanned maneuver. It is the gravest and shameful sin, where the most platonic relationship is shattered by an extreme pervert nefarious act of nonetheless but one's own father. The moral values of an individuals of the society have gone down to sucha level that every day we hear similar news which shudders our mind and should we have become accustomed to saying that females are not safe outside the house, but few such cases like this it is seen that they are not even safe inside their homes, where the epitome of Gods' beautiful creation, a child is ravished by her own father for his momentary sexual needs and pleasure which is heart rendering odious.

3. The change would not merely come from increasing publicizing giving harsher punishments etc. but required change lies in upgrading the moral values inside all of us and imbibing an essential value that women are not object of sexual gratification. The barbarity of the offence of rape cannot by over emphasized especiallywhen we have witnessed

the most gruesome and horrific instances of the same in the recent pasts. The indifference that was created towards feral men with quotation reporting of rape was followed a furor bringing the heinousness and depravity of the offence once again in to forefront, awakening yet hither to do dormant attitude of the society. On flipping of the pages of the News Paper or to the channels of the Television the only resonating sound is a new incident of rape. The argument being advanced is that the incidents of rape have been increased manifold but in reality it is also due to the metamorphic change the society is undergoing, that of the new found willing ness of the Survivors to report the offenses rather thanbeing hapless victims like before. However in the face of this positive development. We cannot turn a blind eye to the fact that the consequences of this development.

4. Now the next phase of action to be taken by Court is Punishment and for this Court believe that "The main purpose of punishment is to protect Society by deterring potential offenders by preventing the social offender from committing further offences and by referring and turning him into law-abiding citizen.

When a person commits a crime and is punished by the State, there are four main purposes of the punishment: retribution incapacitation deterrenceand rehabilitation. Retribution involves inflectional painuponoffenders through imprisonment or same or method of punishment that makes them 'pay their debt to Society' by their harmful action.

In Capacitation is the direct result of incarceration which offenders are imprisoned by which society large is protected from their potential actions.

Deterrence may be divided into two categories, general deterrence and specific deterrence. General deterrence is aimed at the Public, which sees the punishment inflicted upon offenders and avoid actions that might have the same consequences for the criminal actions. Specified deterrence uses the painful consequences of punishment to discourage convicted offenders from repeating their criminal behaviors.

With Rehabilation the criminal justice attempts to change the behavior of offenders and transform them into productive and law abiding citizens. Unlike retribution rehabilitation focuses on the offender rather than the offence. Attempts are made to discover the cause of a convicted offender's criminal behavior and to treat the behavior through correctional program. The ultimate goal of rehabilitation of the interrogation of offenders into the society. This philosophy of punishment dominated correctional policy and practice for over 70 years of Independence. In this case the rehabilitation the criminal justice is more to its ability.

JUDGEMENT

The present appeal has been preferred by the Appellant under section 374 (2) of the code of Criminal procedure, 1973,herein after referred to as Criminal Penal code challenging the impugned judgment in order on sentence dt.15.4 2010 and 29 4. 2010 respectively passed by the Learned Trial court there by convicting the appellant for committing the offense of rape under Section 376ofIPC Act and sentencing him to undergo Life imprisonment and also to pay fine of Rs. 5000/- in default thereof to undergo simple imprisonment for a period of six months U/S 376 of IPV, 1860 (herein after referred to an IPC) and also sentenced him undergo rigorous imprisonment for two years for offence punishable under section 506 (i) of IPC. Both the offence to run concurrently.Concurrently withthis Judgment The Court also found that the culprit was a drug addict and marketing it for curing the certain ailments and used for his self-campaign of Sex ride over innocent and minor girls which attracts the provisions of Section 17and 275 of Indian Penal code which also accord punishment Imprisonment for a period of one year and payment Rs.5000 as a penalty. Thus in total the court hereby passed decree of life time imprisonment added with another year for Drug usage.

The three daughters, named Lakshmi, Saraswathi and Durga are hereby exonerated with honor even though they had committed a crime of mutilating the organs of culprit as he was indulging the culprit for committing adultery with the 4 years small child of their brother Seetha Ram. However, they have shown great heart touching humanity for tolerating the offense committed by their father which is really applaud able for maintaining silence all along." Judge also asserted further as this is a clear case of assault committed by the father of thechildren's and this fact has been accepted by the Culprit. This court does not hold any view for recommending of higher court's review in this regard as it would be superfluous in the stand of the decision taken by the this court.

Ramanujam while obeying for the decree the Judge passed went along with police which took him to central Jail in Rajahmundry itself"

Most of the attendants in the court appreciated the tolerance and magnanimity shown towards the convict and got simply subdued with atrocities. Office members including Collectorate staff attended the court and gave a clap to Durga for her tolerance subdued during her tender age and praised for her tolerance and silence over family atrocities.

Seetha Ram could not show his face to his sisters. He became more emotional and wanted to kill his father for spoiling so many lives including his sisters and wife. Lakshmi made to cool and forget the convict. You should have informed me I would have Siva's Trident and used to kill him totally by crashing it in his heart and gone surrendered to the police. He conveyed his sorry to Venkat and prostrated and touched the feet of Kondiah and Uoormila and submitted his mistakes for condolence transferred his thanks for giving courage and shelter to her sisters to move on to develop their career. They both innocently said "No Seetha Ram it is them who stood like hill without retreat in the Tempest of Tsunami. They are our virtual daughters and converted our barren field to evergreen spring. We are proud of them too.

Then Venkat said "Hey Hello! You telling as if I am not related to you as a son." All laughed at him and said you are naughty boy"

The marriages of all the three, Lakshmi, Saraswathi and Durga was celebrated with the Groom Trio Venkat, Chiranjeevi and Ajay. The parents of these Trio, Anjaiah, Koteeswara Rao and Ramanna Choudhary felt very happy without considering the fact that there daughter-in-laws are spoiled one. All the three along with society male members took an oath to take every possible step in getting eradicated another such evils of casteism and spoiled women or used women prevailed in the Indian society since ages.

|| *SHUBHAM-SARVEJAN SUKHINO BHAVATHU*||

www.ingramcontent.com/pod-product-compliance
Lightning Source LLC
Chambersburg PA
CBHW031111020726
47495CB00007B/2155